HOLLOW
BIBLE

By
CONNOR DE BRULER

MONTAG

Montag Press ISBN: 978-1-957010-15-1
Design © 2022 Amit Dey

Montag Press Team:

Cover: Rick Febre
Author Photo: Ron Candella
Editor: Charlie Franco
Managing Director: Charlie Franco

A Montag Press Book
www.montagpress.com
Montag Press
777 Morton Street, Unit B
San Francisco CA 94129 USA

Montag Press, the burning book with the hatchet cover, the skewed word mark and the portrayal of the long-suffering fireman mascot are trademarks of Montag Press.

Printed & Digitally Originated in the United States of America
10 9 8 7 6 5 4 3 2 1

For The Bobby Lees.

"Hollow Bible elevates the lurid subject matter from glamorized shock to real poetry...a thorny vine that grows through a lava field. Violence, drugs, and filth, de Bruler does it better than most."

"Try to look away."

"Recognize without testing it, the evil there, in your bed, your chest, your thighs, and forsaken feet, like those on a crucifix…"

— Pasolini

1

Last night I had a dream that I worked in a modern office where people got to wear whatever they wanted; the kinds of clothes young rich people wear on Friday nights in bustling downtowns, all beards and beanies, and girls in peasant skirts. I made decent money and I enjoyed what I did there. I think we wrote marketing copy for computer sales. My boss was kind. My coworkers were kind. Everyone was happy. I had done a good job writing a pitch that morning and my coworkers decided to take me to lunch at an upscale sushi bar. We laughed about mundane things and talked about things to do on our weekends off in the city.

After that, I woke up. The storm outside was raging. Dead palm leaves crashed against my motel-room window. There was a group of marines in the suite beside me, taking refuge from the hurricane, drinking, and playing music. I sat up in bed and took another valium and chased it with tequila and tried to remember how good I had it in my dream.

2

'm gonna lay this out as best I can, and you can decide for yourself what it is I'm guilty of.

My name is Basil Shaver. I get my name from my grandfather. I don't know how old I am. I'm guessing...early thirties. It's hard to tell when you've been beaten up over the years as many times as I have. I've done a lot of hard drugs too and I still booze and smoke, which doesn't help either. Maybe...late twenties? Who knows?

I know where I come from: Brazil, Indiana. I don't know if I was born there because I don't have a birth certificate, but I remember living there for a while when I was real little. I lived with my mother and a distant uncle. There's only one famous person I can think of that also came out of Brazil and that was Jimmy Hoffa. It's fitting that I come from the same place as him. Everyone from Brazil disappears eventually.

My grandfather was black. My grandmother was white. They never got married. The state still had laws against it until about 1948. At least, that's what my uncle told me. My grandfather worked at a full-service gas station on the Clay County Line.

He was working late in the evening when a rowdy group of youngsters drove up in an International pickup and told him to fill up the tank. He filled it up and they started yelling at him, saying they only needed a dollar's worth. He called them liars and got the owner involved. The owner came out with his double-barrel buckshot which persuaded them to pay up. It was a fatal mistake. Things were quiet for another week or so. That's how my uncle told it. It was late on a Wednesday night in August when three trucks surrounded the little station. It was a posse of Klan members who drove down from Kokomo just to see my grandfather. They killed the owner first. He was found between the front door and the gas pumps, lying in the dust, with multiple exit wounds to his chest and back from four different pistol calibers. My grandfather wasn't heard from again and his body was never found. That was the beginning of the end for my lineage. We've been losing ever since.

I'm only a quarter black. Most people think I'm Italian or Turkish, and by people, I mean low lives and johns. I've heard a lot of random theories: Cherokee, Jewish, Armenian.

My mother was fifteen when I was born. My father was probably in his forties. I never met him. We lived for a few years in Brazil and after that, we moved to Indianapolis. It was in that cramped apartment on Muskett Street where my mother first tried to drown me in the bathtub. My uncle wasn't around to placate her anymore, and I was afraid to go home every day after school. She had a couple of different boyfriends. One of them was a pretty nice guy, but he didn't stick around long. It was the really bad guy who won out. He moved in and pushed me aside. They did things together like extinguishing cigarette butts on my skin. About a year later, I was abandoned at the Circle

Center Mall downtown. I wasn't a teenager yet, but I wasn't a child either. It was night. The storefronts were shutting down. I stared through the tall glass windows at the cold neon glare of the city. After wandering around looking for them, a security guard caught me. He must have thought I was older because he didn't take me to an office and try to contact my parents. Instead, he escorted me to the back entrance and kicked me off the premises. I just zipped up my coat and wandered down the street. I've been on the run ever since.

I stole from restaurants and unattended purses in the city park for about a week. I practically lived in the basement of a comic book store, pulling fifty-cent issues of The Mask and Batman: No Man's Land from their plastic sleeves to read in secret until the clerk found me down there and kicked me out. I wasn't on my own for long. An old pedophile named Harry bought me a hotdog one day and asked me why I wasn't in school. I told him my mom didn't want me anymore. It was music to his ears. He told me about a place he could take me with other kids my age, but I had to be okay with driving down to Kentucky with him. He was nice. He was well-dressed. I was already trying to dodge the truant officer, so I agreed. He met me the next day at the public library in a Chevy Astro. There was an older girl in the passenger's seat who put me at ease. She must have been seventeen. She had red hair and a belly-button ring and chain-smoked Salems. I was obsessed with her Zippo lighter and she let me play with it. We drove down to Kentucky listening to rock music and hip-hop on the radio. Eminem's *Lose Yourself* had just come out and it played non-stop on every station.

Things changed once we crossed the Ohio River into Louisville. The girl stopped talking as much and Harry started asking me questions that I didn't know how to answer. As a kid, I just tried to shrug them off.

"I don't know anything about that kind of stuff," I said.

"What? You don't have any girlfriends or boyfriends back in Indy? You never kissed anybody before?"

"Boyfriends? No, man. I'm not gay."

"How do you know if you never tried it?" he said. "And there's nothing wrong with being gay. Lots of people are gay. Why don't you give her a kiss first and then kiss me and decide which one you like better? Some people like both."

I started to get scared.

We stopped at a gas station and I wanted to get out and pick my own soda, but Harry wouldn't let me. He asked us what we wanted so he could get it. He filled up the gas tank and left us in the van. That was the first time I thought about making a run for it, but I didn't. Stupid decision.

The girl, the redhead, I still can't remember her name, was the one who made the first pass. It was all an elaborate plan. She got me calm (as calm as I was going to get) so Harry could take over. She unzipped my pants and pushed me to the back of the van. Harry came in a few minutes later. They both raped me in the parking lot of the gas station in broad daylight. I could have yelled for help, but I didn't. I didn't think anyone would help me. I didn't think anything like that could happen to anyone.

We drove the rest of the way and I didn't say a word. I wasn't the same person after that. I hear a lot of people talk about it like something had been taken away from them. It felt to me more like they had put something on me, an invisible suit that I'd have to wear for the rest of my life. I was an empty vessel before and now I am full of toxins. It was as though I had contracted a disease. Harry put the radio back on but I couldn't hear a damn thing. I was so deep in my head. I wish I could articulate it better, but I can't. I don't think there's enough vocabulary for it.

Harry drove us to a secluded place in the woods of Kentucky. I had no idea where we were. He drove us to a clearing and we waited for a man in a pickup truck to roll up. The guy wore camouflage and had a thick mustache. He handed Harry a stack of money and I was told to get in the back of his truck. It was that simple. It was like buying a horse and I'd already been broken too.

I could describe the terrible things that happened afterward but it wouldn't make me feel any better to write it down, to immortalize it. Some don't even have the imagination to invent what I've experienced. No fire-and-brimstone sermon has ever stirred me.

I spent a few days chained up in a barn where I was fed pizza crusts and trough water meant for horses. I was raped every night almost all night long.

On the final day, he unchained me and let me take a shower, and even gave me some new clothes. A man and woman came to the house while I was eating eggs at the kitchen table. They had strange accents and talked to me like they were going to be my new parents. Their names were Oksana and Piotyr: scouts for the Chechens. They haggled over my price with the farmer and took me away in their Land Cruiser. Oksana told me things weren't going to be so bad anymore. That I had been through a lot. That I was brave. That I had the potential to be somebody. That they weren't going to abandon me. That they wanted me to be a part of their family.

We were on the highway for a long time. When night rolled around, they gave me a pill to sleep. I passed out instantly. When I came to, I was groggier than I had ever been. It was like being resurrected. I was a zombie. It was raining and we were far, far away from Kentucky. I could tell by the look of the land. Palmettos lined the streets. Big signs for diners, saloons, and surf shops crowded the skyline. Tourists passed the crosswalks with their bright umbrellas. I asked if we were in Hollywood.

Piotyr laughed.

"No," he said. "This is South Carolina. We're on the coast."

Everything was different here and I wondered how happy I was going to be. I was so groggy everything felt like a dream.

We drove off the main drag and into the swamp and marsh of the backwoods where alligators sunned on the banks of the scum-covered ponds and estuarial lowlands, deep into the heart of the dark jungle-like terrain where Spanish moss hung from the ancient oaks. We crossed a gate and followed a narrow dirt path up to the antebellum mansion. They showed me to my room up the winding stairs and padlocked the door behind me. I shared a room with two other boys who immediately beat me up.

3

worked in the bordello for years. They liked me because I
didn't complain and I didn't argue. I got fewer beatings for
that. I had a bad case of Stockholm Syndrome. When I aged
out of hustling, I had developed enough trust with Oksana and
Piotyr that they moved me to the side business: dope. Dope
became half my world. Looking back, I was crazy lucky not
to have tried heroin. I'd be dead if I had ever touched smack.
Smack made you even more of a slave than you already were
and it also made people unpredictable. You didn't want your
delivery boy beholden to the H-train. It was bad business.
Heaven on the opposite end of a spike. People die every day. I'd
pop a Percocet from time to time, but I was partial to coke. I
still am. I had lost myself already at this point, running drugs for
the Chechens across the tourist stops on the SC coast. My lon-
gest run was from Savannah, Georgia to Willmington, North
Carolina. We hit Myrtle Beach almost every day, Hilton Head,
Beaufort, Kiawah Island, St. Pawleys…

The second half of my world became Itandehui. We called
her Ita for short. She was a Mexican girl snatched off the streets

of Oaxaca. She'd been through Texas, Louisiana, Mississippi, Florida. You name it. I liked her. We used to cut up all the time. Hang out. Smoke weed and do lines together. We both had matching brands on our thighs: ₽. It was the Russian Ruble sign. That was their trademark. That meant we were property.

Ita always had a bruise or two across her face because she didn't get along with Oksana and Piotyr like I did. I vouched for her as much as I could. I had gotten accustomed to taking a punch like it was nothing, but Oksana knew how to hurt me. I had to watch whenever they tortured Ita. That always left a sick feeling in the pit of my stomach.

Itandehui aged out around the same time as me. Instead of selling her to a street pimp, they kept her in the legit club. It was a miserable existence.

I was already getting to the end of my rope running coke and meth all day every day for the next few years. I imagine it was like being a trucker with no days off. I didn't have my own money. I had nowhere to go. I was stuck right where they wanted me. I did what I could to visit Ita at the gentleman's club but the cover charge usually cleaned me out and after I'd talk to her for a few minutes the bouncers would eighty-six me for bothering the girls.

I came up with a plan to see her. The Chechens rented an apartment in the area where they stashed girls. The club bouncers swapped shifts to guard them like prisoners. Some of them were diehard watchmen and girls didn't even brush their teeth without the go-ahead. But a few of them weren't so keen. I cased the place two nights in a row, watching the shift changes, noting when the car pulled in to take the girls to the club in the morning. I sat in Piotyr's car the first night and watched from the bushes like a sniper on the second in case they got wise. I didn't go back on the third night. It didn't seem right. I had to play this smart. I started to think about what might happen if I botched it. They might beat me to a pulp, cut off one of my toes, touch up the old brand... Maybe. It was more likely they'd hurt Ita.

I was driving back from a routine drop at a title loan front, eating a breakfast burrito in a brand new Toyota Oksana had leased to move some weight when I realized that the only thing I cared about anymore was Ita. Ever since she left the bordello, I began to suffer. I was grieving her absence and she wasn't even dead. Maybe that's what you'd call love. But love was a dirty word for a seasoned prostitute. Love was at best a sick euphemism in the sex trade. Since I was a child, hundreds of men told me they loved me before and after they ejaculated. The same guys wouldn't think twice to choke you until you passed out. I couldn't say this temporary obsession was love, but it was the most significant experience of my life up to that point. And no, it wasn't healthy. But nothing about my existence was. If I did one good thing in my life, it was going to be saving her from that apartment in Beaufort.

Piotyr was waiting for me when I got back to the mansion. I tossed him the duffle bag. He unzipped it and stared at the money.

"Seek and ye shall prosper," I said.

"You're a loyal footsoldier, B," he said. "Why don't you take it to the club tonight for processing."

That was his word for money laundering.

"You want me to make the drop?"

"Gotta learn sometime," he said and tossed the bag back in the truck.

I put a cigarette between my lips and we bumped fists.

The place was called Rico's. A Serbian named Alosh ran it for them. He was an old guy with silver hair and four jet-black rectangle tattoos across his arms hiding the evidence of his past war crimes. People said he'd been hiding out in the Southeast since the late 90s.

I walked inside with the duffle bag and told Javier I was making the drop for Piotyr that night. He cocked his head to the side as if I were speaking Swedish.

"Nobody makes a drop besides Piotyr or Oksana," he said.

"Piotyr just gave me a promotion. I'm an exec now. You can tell Alosh. I'm here and I got the money."

He took me to the back office and I sat down across from Alosh's desk. I waited for a long time. They were trying to sweat me, but I just sat there as calm as I'd ever been. Alosh and a few of the money men walked inside. I kicked the bag across the floor. He stopped it with his foot.

"I know you," he said. "You're Oksana's old-time butt boy."

"I'm here to make the money drop for the night," I said, ignoring him.

The floor speakers permeated the drywall with a muted pulse, filling the silence between us. He relented and picked up the bag.

"Follow me," he said, taking me to the counting room.

The operation was not tight. It was downright sloppy. You could barely see the tabletops. There were so many liquor bottles, ashtrays, coke mirrors, and loaded guns amid the stacks of wrinkled cash. It was a parody image from a law textbook on probable cause.

"Sit down," he said, pulling out a chair for me.

They offered me vodka and cognac while they counted the money and started distributing it into different stacks.

I asked if Ita was working that night.

Alosh shook his head as he lit a cigarette.

I didn't push it after that. They divided up the cash and mixed it in with several hauls and refilled the duffle bag with the clean money. The whole thing might have only taken ten minutes if they hadn't stopped to tell jokes and do shots together. They kept offering me shot after shot. I spit out half of them. They didn't notice. The floor was already sticky.

Alosh didn't give me the bag right after filling it. Instead, he patted me on the shoulder and told me to follow him to another room again. I had to play the game, so I went with him. He took me outside by the dumpster. I could hear the cicadas. The concrete backlot was covered in brown magnolia leaves that crunched beneath our feet.

"What are we doing out here?"

"You still want to know where Ita is?"

"What?"

"You heard what I said. You wanna know where she is or not?"

"Where is she?"

"She's safe," he said, smiling. "She's with Piotyr and Oksana."

What happened next is still a blur. Alosh reached into his coat for a snub-nosed revolver. I kicked him in the groin and lifted his hand high so he couldn't aim. We fought for a while.

He managed to get in a few hefty sucker-punches, but he dropped the pistol.

I picked it up.

After I killed him, I ran back into the counting room and started shooting. When I was empty, all I had to do was grab another gun off the table. The smoke cleared. My ears were on fire. Everyone was dead except me. I stood there in awe of what I had just done, a pistol in both hands, shaking. Slowly, the club beat took the place of my tinnitus. I grabbed the bag and filled it with more money and guns and walked out of the club. No one stopped me.

I had to scrap my plan. I drove back to the mansion. I could still hear the pulsating base of the strip club music as I walked around to the secret basement entrance of the bordello. I had two guns which I carried like a child; two giant, pitch-black automatic pistols. I was prepared to die, but I had thought I was going to die every day for years. It made no difference.

I walked up the stairs to the kitchen where I could hear Oksana's voice. I moved into the vestibule area and found her with Ita.

I'm not going to write down what she was doing to her.

I shot Oksana four times and hurried to free Ita. Again, I can't say what she was doing. I had to pull things out of her and unbind other things so she could walk. There was a significant amount of blood. As we left, Big Joe, the bordello's security lookout, turned the corner. I shot him in the throat and he fell against the wall, gargling, bleeding out. I wanted to kill Piotyr too, but he wasn't there and we had to get the fuck out of dodge.

4

We drove like crazy before stopping at a drugstore. I bought Ita gauze, cotton balls, ibuprofen, Neosporin, Cortisone, and a Gatorade. I got myself a screwdriver to swap license plates with a similar make and model. No one caught me.

Ita wasn't hysterical. She was tired, but she kept a smile on her face. She was tough. Both of us were. I turned on the radio and we watched the sunrise through the windshield. There would come a time when we'd have to talk about our situation, but this wasn't it. I held the steering wheel with one hand and held her close with the other. She just smiled and gathered her strength. Neither of us said a word that morning. There was an oldies marathon on the coastal station; soft, happy songs we had never heard before. Every other car on the road and every bird in the sky seemed to cheer us on as we drove west. I wish I could have frozen that moment.

We stopped in a small town with a forgettable name where she cajoled a motel clerk to give us a room facing the parking lot. Ita had a forged American Passport that we used as our photo I.D. under the name Rene Loqeullos. I carried a fake Nevada driver's license under the name Jeb Ruggins. We got some sleep and cleaned ourselves up. I went out to a Walmart and got us some clothes. We'd look like beach town tourists. She was smarter than me and sent me back out for hair color and clippers. We ate drive-thru cheeseburgers and smoked Marlboro menthols that night. There was a Western on the cable channel and I showed her the guns and money I had stolen from the club. That's when it sank in that Piotyr was after us and by extension the whole of the mafia along with other Russian and Latin American contacts. We were still slaves in their eyes, lost pieces of property. All of our underground connections were useless because everyone dealt with the syndicate from Miami to Brighton Beach.

Ita shaved my head and I helped her bleach her hair.

We left in the morning. I wore sunglasses and a floppy hat. She had shimmering, beautiful blonde hair against her dark hazel skin and wide, thick-rimmed shades to hide the bruised edge of her left eye. Once we were on the road, she reached into the bag and unloaded one of the dark pistols like she'd handled the gun a thousand times before, popping the chambered cartridge out the slide, catching the magazine as it dropped out the handle to count the rounds.

"We should stop at a gun shop today," she said.

"How come?"

"These guns are dirty," she said. "They're likely to jam. Need to pick up a bottle of Hoppe's No.9. Get more cartridges too."

"How do you know all that?"

"Tricks," she said. "Gangsters don't maintain their guns the way Southern rednecks do."

I rolled down the window and lit a cigarette.

"You wanna listen to the radio?"

"Sure."

"Mariachi station?"

"Fuck you."

We laughed and I turned it to a rock station. The sun was bright as hell. We turned on the AC and rolled up the windows.

"Where are we gonna go?"

"You wanna go to Mexico?"

"How are we gonna get into Mexico?"

"We can bribe our way in."

"No, I don't wanna go there," she said. "Mexico's how I got here in the first place. They'll expect us to cross some kind of border, plus they got more people down there than up here. I say we stay in the U.S. No one expects us to stay. This country's a maze. Anyone can get lost."

She was right.

We got close to the northern state line and tried to get a nice hotel room this time, as nice as I could find. I proposed a game plan, that we alternate between nicer hotels and methadone roadhouses. It would be harder for them to track us that way. But we didn't know what we were doing. We were like children. No reputable hotel would book out a room without a credit card to place on hold. No one on the other side of life understood us. The polite clerk at the checkout desk in the hotel with a water fountain in the lobby looked at us like she was staring at a pair of walking mugshots. A stack of wrinkled cash said trouble to everyone. She got on the phone and whispered as she spoke. Ita looked at me and we split out the front. I watched our backs in the parking lot to make sure no one got the license number and vehicle description. Scared, we shot out of there and drove all night. Once there were enough miles between us and the city, we calmed down and even laughed about it. Funny thing was, we'd both been to hotels just about that nice or better for johns and orgies and underground, Russian-financed pornography when were kids. We didn't have any reason to think there were different rules. Far as we knew, all hotels were the same as a person's lifespan. It could be a hellhole or a haven. I might have laughed to ease the pain, but I was terrified to think about all the parts of life I knew nothing about.

Ita scored us some good speed from a trucker in a gas station Burger King and we kept going until our eyes were bloodshot and our hands vibrated like the truck's engine. We got a dark and dingy room above a failing dinner franchise. It was only one in the afternoon when we sat down at the bar but it might as well have been three in the morning for us. We figured alcohol would even us out from being wired for so long. The bartender gave us a couple of menus and drink specials that didn't apply to the time of day. I got Tequila over ice and Ita drank straight Jack Daniels. I ordered a plate of wings and Ita tore into a rare steak that was more gristle than meat. We did a few shots of some blue crap and staggered back to our room. We lay side by side in bed. She fell asleep first and I watched her breathe in peace before I passed out.

We woke up the next day, checked out of the room, and groggily crossed the boulevard to the Circle K where I filled up the tank and got us both coffee. I drank mine black. She put cream and sugar in hers. They even had a little shaker of cinnamon which she poured into her coffee as well. It looked like a pile of dirt on the surface. I bought a six-pack of beer, beef jerky, two bananas, a fresh hard pack of cigarettes, and a road map. I remember all of these details because they're all I have. Every moment we spent together, we were inventing ourselves. It was like being born. We smoked in the truck while we drank our coffee. I pulled over onto a dirt shoulder of a secluded country road after passing the interstate signs and looked to see where we were. Ita suggested we get a couple of burner phones sooner rather than later and I agreed with her. We were close to a little blink-and-miss hamlet called Crab Orchard in West Virginia. I figured we'd follow the same road north to MacArthur and get on the highway again.

"You wanna go to Ohio?" I said.

"What's in Ohio?"

"I don't know."

"Yeah, sure. Let's go to Ohio."

We were improvising. I think we just liked being in the car. Moving felt safe. It started to rain. I turned on the windshield wipers. Ita rolled down her window and reached out her hand to feel the droplets on her skin.

I asked her how her wounds were doing.

"I'm healing," she said. "It itches. Everything is scabbed over. As long as I keep putting antibiotic cream on it, I should be okay."

There weren't any cops on the road, so he had a couple of beers and tossed the glass bottles out the window. The dark sky looked like a pile of trash bags. Ita noted how creepy all the farmhouses looked.

We drove through Crab Orchard which had a quaint little downtown, like something out of a movie where nothing that bad ever happened.

"You think we could ever start again? Get some normal jobs at a grocery store and just be normal people?"

"You mean if Piotyr wasn't coming for us?" I said. "Sure. I'd like that."

"You'd think we might crack and throw it all away?"

"I don't know," I said.

The rain cleared up and we headed straight for MacArthur.

5

We stopped on the outskirts of some giant county garbage dump in Ohio. It was the first time I had ever seen seagulls so far inland. It was like they had followed us from the coast.

"Do you think they come in from the great lakes or something?"

"I don't know," Ita said, loading the magazine with .45 ACP cartridges. She had a whole set up on the hood of the truck with fresh ammunition and the guns I had stolen. I lined up a few empty Heineken bottles on a distant pillar and propped up an old armchair. Ita said she was going to teach me how to shoot and reload.

"Alright," she said. "First thing's first. Is this gun loaded?"

I saw her take the magazine out.

"No, not anymore."

"Trick question," she said and shot out one of the bottles. "There was one in the chamber, but you didn't know that. How can you tell?"

I shrugged.

"Trick question. You can't. All guns are always loaded all the time. Treat every gun like it's hot."

She slid the magazine back in and handed me the pistol. I took a few shots at the armchair and the beer bottles and once I got used to reloading I set the .45 down. My wrist was sore. I was better with Alosh's revolver, a snub nose .357 magnum.

Ita was a better shot than I was.

"Who the hell taught you about guns?"

"Got to have something to talk about with the johns. Guns is a pretty common subject."

"Yeah, you said that, but I'm not sure I believe you. What Johns are gonna take a girl to the range with him and get her used to shootin'?"

"You don't need to know everything about my past," she said.

"What past? We're the same age."

"Yeah, and how old are you exactly?"

I went silent. I didn't know my age.

"That's what I thought," she said. "I learned about guns once. Let's leave it at that."

We practiced shooting for another few minutes when a Jeep rolled up behind us. I thought they were security guards at first, but it was just two guys in hunting jackets. They looked young and kind of skinny. I could see a shotgun rack holding a Mossberg pump-action through the windshield.

"Y'all shootin' guns out here?" the kid yelled from the window of the jeep, a cigarette dangling from his mouth.

I didn't like the way he looked and I was ready for a fight.

"Yeah," I said, the revolver in my hand.

"Well, there's people down the way complaining. You better get out of here 'fore the cops come," he said and rolled up the window. The jeep backed up and turned around.

Ita packed everything and made sure the guns had their safeties on. We drove away. I never heard any sirens. I wasn't sure if someone had really called the cops or if they were just trying to get rid of us. Either way, the boys didn't mess with us.

6

I can hear the rain pounding against the catwalk railing outside my door. Sometimes, at night, it drowns out the television and the people fighting through the walls. The streets are flooded and the bridges are out. The winter homes of rich, out-of-state Kentuckian horse breeders are slipping into the ocean and the historic lands of the first enslaved Africans in the New World are disappearing in the tides. After all that's happened, I'm back on the coast. The hurricane winds seep through the cracks in the doorframe to my lonely room and whip against my feet as I write this down. I've got some food with me that I bought from the Piggily Wiggly down the street before everything shut down. I've also got a supply of booze and dope. I imagine I've got enough rations to last me another four days. A long time, all things considered.

I apologize if you're reading this. You're not in the best hands. I'm not much of a writer. I'm sure there are mistakes and overused cliches. It is what it is. Hell. Who am I kidding? You're not reading all of it. If anything, you're a cop and you're skimming through this jumbled text to find a confession, to find out who to charge with a crime. I don't care. If all this rambling crap does is help you put away a few people from the organized criminal groups involved, maybe save one kid off the street, then it'll have been for something.

7

We stayed in Ohio for a couple of days playing house before moving on to Indiana. I wanted to show Ita where I was from but she was tired and wanted to get a drink and crash out for a day off the road. I found a motel on a back road a couple of miles outside of Indianapolis called the Gin Diamond Inn in the midst of the soy fields. The place was shaped like a giant arch with a shimmering, emerald green sign and looked like the setting of an unfinished dream. I parked in the gravel lot outside the main office and paid the clerk for a room. He gave me a key and explained how to drive on through the archway under the green light to the rooms which stood independent of one another as little huts.

We crashed on the creaky bed and stretched our legs, sharing a bottle of Hennessy, smoking even though we weren't supposed to smoke in the room. Ita got drunker than I had seen her get in a while. She started talking about clients, jobs, Johns that said they'd take her away from all of this and never did, her parents in Oaxaca, and what Oksana had done to her. She got angry at me for telling her to shut up and locked herself in the bathroom with the bottle. I told her I was sorry. She told me I was worse than some of the lying Johns she had serviced.

"How is that? I'm not lying to you."

"You got me in this mess. You think we can drive around and spend stolen money and live like nothing's wrong."

"I don't think that, Ita," I said.

"They're gonna find us. They're gonna find us and torture us and put our bodies in ten-gallon drums."

"We're not going to let that happen," I said, half-believing it myself.

"You just want to fuck me. You just want me for yourself. You're just like them, paying to live in a fantasy for a little while."

"I'm not living in a fantasy," I said. "Look around you. Look where we are. This is real."

She stopped talking after that. I could hear her crying. It took me a few minutes to pick the lock on the door. I opened it slowly. I told her I was sorry again.

It wasn't the first time I found her cutting herself, but it might have been the worst. In that short time, she managed to slash her wrists, carve the word slave into her arm, and slice into part of her thigh brand. I don't know where she got the razor. Someone must have left it in the room because the bottle was intact. She was naked inside the dry shower nook. There was blood all over the dirty tile. I wrapped up her hands in the leftover gauze I bought from the store that first night, but the bleeding wouldn't stop. I went back into the room and picked up the motel phone. It was a tough decision but I ended up calling an ambulance.

When they took her away, the EMTs told me the cuts in her wrists had stopped bleeding. They weren't particularly deep.

"They looked deep to me," I said.

The EMTs weren't the main guys I had to talk to. It was a cop. A white guy with a military haircut. He wasn't so bad. He didn't ask to look around the room. He didn't ask for my driver's license either, he just asked me for a statement. I told him we were from South Carolina, coming back from visiting family in Michigan. I told him Ita was having problems with her mother. When you're a kid getting passed around different places, shuttled into dark hotel rooms, crossing the street alone in the middle of the night, you learn how to tell a convincing lie. The cop bought my story and didn't ask me to corroborate anything. I asked where they were taking Ita.

"Community Hospital North," he said.

The EMT corrected him before closing the back door to the ambulance.

"IU Health Methodist."

The cop repeated the name and explained what a 72-hour hold was.

When everyone had left, the clerk came to me with a refund and told me to leave the motel. At least he gave me my money back.

The hospital was in the middle of the city. God knows why they took her there. The security guard let me in the parking garage when I told him my wife was in the ICU. He just waved me on through. I parked in a dark corner and took a nap in the truck. In the morning when the nurses were heading through the automatic doors with their packed lunches, I got out of the truck and stretched my legs. I went inside and bought a coffee from the downstairs cafe and watched all the normal people talk about high school football and girls' volleyball and book clubs like I was in some kind of movie.

I wandered around the hospital until the afternoon when I found the right ward and asked the woman at the front desk about my "wife" and the 72-hour hold. I waited in a cramped dark lobby for a long time before a nurse came out and talked to me about coming back after a day or so for an update. I was polite and agreed.

After that, I went to the Children's museum and killed the rest of the day like a weirdo looking at dinosaur bones and stuffed Timber wolves.

When I went back to the hospital to discharge her, a little Indian doctor took me aside and asked about the mark on her thigh. My face went red.

"I'm not an idiot," he said. "I've seen symbols branded into flesh like that before."

"I'm not her pimp. We were both working," I said and showed him my brand. "We aren't in the life anymore. I got us out of that. I'm just trying to help her."

He looked defeated and shrugged. They discharged her and told me she was groggy from a mood stabilizer. The doctor told me to keep her away from sharp objects and not to let her drink alcohol again. We wheeled her out to the garage and put her in the truck.

I took out my screwdriver and switched license plates in a Kroger parking lot.

I drove south out of instinct and remembered that first drive I took with Harry and the girl. I lit a cigarette and smoked it down to the filter. Ita stared at her bandaged hands.

"What did you tell them?" she said.

"Me? Nothing. What did you say to the psych doctor?"

She didn't look at me.

"What psych doctor?"

"Nobody talked to you about why you cut yourself up?"

"Yeah," she said. "Someone came in and read me questions off a piece of paper."

"That's it?"

"There was a person who watched me. Even when I took a shower. That was about it. How much did it cost us?" she said.

"Don't worry about it. I took care of it."

"We're running out of money," she said. "We can't live like this for the rest of our lives."

"I know," I said. "We'll figure something out."

"We better figure it out quick."

"I thought we were gonna find a little town somewhere out in the plains and get normal jobs?"

"Is that your fantasy?" she said. "You wanna live in a little white house on a hill with a tire swing in the front yard?"

"What's wrong with that?"

"They don't let people like us live that way. It's impossible."

"It's not impossible."

"Even if we make it. One day a guy with the same kind of tattoos as Piotyr is gonna show up and cut your eyelids off so you can't blink while he fucks me to death with a tire iron."

I didn't say anything after that. I just thought to myself in silence.

She leaned back and fell asleep.

8

I remembered my old plan in Kentucky and told her about it in Tennessee. She didn't think I was serious.

"That's just another fantasy, pie in the sky."

I pulled the car over and spread out the map on the dashboard and then took a pen and started circling points on the map.

"What are you doing?"

"Do you remember what I used to do for them, for Piotyr and Oksana?"

She shook her head.

"Random pickups?"

"I started to do more than that. They trusted me. I moved weight and I moved cash. I was on the road all day every day for a long time."

"Okay, so?"

"I know more than they should have told me. See these points on the map?"

She nodded.

"I memorized the maps behind Piotyr's desk. These are car title loan stores."

"You see them everywhere."

"These are the ones they use to launder money. It isn't just the strip club. There's a whole interwoven network along the coast of these payday advance stops. They use them as banks. And I know about every one."

"And?"

"And what? We know where their money is. Let's take it."

"They're already after us, why are we taking more?"

"That's my point. They're coming after us one way or another. I say we hit'em where it hurts."

She went silent.

I folded up the map and pulled onto the road. We drove through the mountains. The stone walls on the side of the spiraling interstate were lined with tall cages to protect the cars from stray boulders falling off the ridge. Every passing town was nestled in the bottom of a smoky valley and looked like the kind of place you only knew about if you lived there. I imagined growing a beard and working in a sawmill for the rest of my life, getting drunk in a forestine trailer park on the weekends, and dying happy in my fifties of lung cancer. Maybe a town like that would take me. But it wasn't in the cards.

"It's suicide," she said out of nowhere.

I hesitated as I slowed the truck around a steep bend.

"They'll kill us anyway," I said. "And look at your arms. We're already killing ourselves."

She said nothing.

We drove for another few miles. She was thinking about it just like I was.

We stopped outside in Knoxville and found a low-rate place on the river beside an abandoned paddle-boat rental. The railroad bridge was the color of dried blood against the dark sky. I stuck my head out the window and smoked a cigarette and drank Hennessy out of a paper cup. Ita sat up in bed and held the ashtray in her hand as she smoked in the flickering light of the TV. The noise of sitcom reruns and car dealership commercials filled the emptiness and loneliness of the room with the sound of fabricated serenity and enthusiasm alike.

"Do you believe in God, Basil?"

I shook my head.

"I don't think I have the capacity to get into that kind of talk right now," I said.

"When did you decide you wanted to get back at Piotyr instead of just run away? Was it after I cut myself up?"

"The apartment you were held at back in Beaufort," I said. "I cased the place for two days, watching from the trees. I planned on busting you out. That's when I first thought about it."

"That's why Oksana tortured me, isn't it? Because they found you out?"

I hung my head and blew smoke toward the floor.

"It isn't just their money," she said. "It's everyone's money."

I crushed the cigarette against the sill.

"But the spots are Piotyr's responsibility. The way I see it, the longer it takes for them to catch us, the deeper in the shit he'll be with the Russians, the Salvadorians, the Albanians... He'll be fucked."

"They'll come after us too," she said.

"I killed everyone in that room back at the club before I stole the guns and the money. We're already in the shit. Let's take some of them with us."

"I'd like to kill him," she said. "Piotyr. I wanna cut his penis off."

"We might not get to kill him ourselves," I said. "But if we destroy their money, he's as good as dead. Even if they get to us after. What we don't spend, we'll just burn or something. It's cash. They'll never get it back. I say we go for it."

"I need to sleep on it," she said.

I took a shower while she watched TV.

I dried off in the bathroom and crawled into bed. We watched a sitcom about a doctor and his wacky patients. I stared through the window at the lights reflecting off the surface of the Tennessee River. Some kind of barge passed beneath the railroad bridge. I turned back the TV as Ita fell asleep and enjoyed the calm of the night.

When I woke up, Ita's side of the bed was empty and the truck keys were gone from the nightstand. I got up and stared out the window at the rain swelling the river. It was a little underwhelming compared to the Ohio but I haven't seen the Mississippi or the Colorado yet. I have a thing for rivers. Maybe I've seen too much of the ocean; those long white-trash beaches facing the ash-colored water of the Atlantic.

I watched the rain and the mist roll off the surface of the river. The sky was gray. The water was gray. All the trees were still. The cars in the parking lot sat there in the downpour as if they hadn't been driven in years. I could feel a calm inside me so alien that I was afraid to trust it. Ita was gone. I hoped she'd have a chance and Piotyr would only send someone to kill me. I started to feel sick when I realized they'd find her if she held onto the truck. The duffle bag full of loose cash and guns sat in the corner of the room. It was still full, so she had no resources.

I got dressed and walked across the street to the gas station for coffee. I trudged through the rain to the wood-paneled awning of the derelict boat rental where I drank my coffee and had a cigarette away from other people. The rain continued to fall. I tossed the butt into a rippling puddle and walked down to the riverbank. I could see a Pepsi logo through the shallow water on the mucky edge. Someone had submerged an entire vending machine. Once I was good and wet, I returned to the room. I figured it was about time to check out. I packed my shit and left the bottle of Hennessy in the corner like an offering at the foot of a shrine. I locked the door and headed out.

A black Fiat Palio pulled up beside me.

I thought two brawny Eastern Europeans were about to pull me into the back.

I turned away until I heard Ita's voice. She was alone in the front seat.

"Get in," she said.

"Where did you get a new ride?"

"Mexicans," she said. "I traded it."

"Is it hot?"

"It's clean enough. No one's looking for it. You think a normal dealership would take a truck from a woman without an I.D.?"

I checked us out of the room and got inside the little Brazilian-made box of a car.

"I thought you left."

"I almost did," she said. "But I don't want to anymore."

"You sure about that?"

"Yeah," she said. "I'm ride-or-die at this point. I was hoping that getting a fresh ride would prove that to you."

"You don't have to prove anything to me," I said.

We hit the highway and I realized I hadn't seen Ita drive before.

"You can drive."

"What made you think I couldn't?"

"I don't know," I said. "You chose a good car. Nondescript. Looks like everything else on the road."

"That's the idea," she said. "You talk a hell of a lot. Why don't you shut up and trust me once in a while? Seems like I know more about the outside world than you."

She was right. She could drive and she knew guns. What did I know? How to count? How to BS my way through a world that didn't want me? I liked to think of Itandehui as my equal. We were from the same world, only she didn't seem to like that thought. I didn't argue with her. I'm not a hot head. I can keep my mouth shut when I need to. I wondered if she could do the same when it came down to it. Maybe, maybe not. Maybe we were both gonna die in a hail of bullets. Either the cops or the Chechens. One way or the other. There's no certainty in this fucked up world and it's a lot harder to accept that once you've finally got something to lose.

"Do you believe in God, Basil?"

"Nope."

9

We hit the first title loan franchise on a Friday evening in Alcoa, Tennessee. The place had neon signs and looked sleazy as all hell. There was a McDonald's across the street. We cased the place while we had breakfast and went back just before closing time. We wore baggy tracksuits we picked up from a local Walmart Supercenter along with ski masks and thick mirrored shades. When we talked, we talked in Eastern European accents. I shot the clock off the wall to show the manager and the young girl behind the front desk that I was crazy. We grabbed the cash and bolted. The Palio was parked two blocks down the road in front of an abandoned VFW building. Slowly, we peeled off the shades and then the masks, and finally, once we hit the back roads, the top halves of the tracksuits.

We got a motel room on the tourist strip in Gatlinburg and went out to a late dinner at a barbecue place. Tennessee barbecue was different from Carolina. They weren't in for the pulled pork as much and pushed the ribs and the tomato-based sauce. I missed the hot mustard. Ita didn't seem to mind. That tiny girl was one hell of a carnivore. I stuck with a sandwich while she put away a whole rack of wet-brushed ribs and four cans of Pabst and a shot of whiskey. We hadn't eaten since six that morning. We paid and left and went outside for a smoke. There were drunk rednecks and loitering teenagers everywhere. Cars passed us blasting music. When we got back to the room, Ita ripped the gauze off her arms and stared at the word 'slave' carved into her skin. It was still pretty legible. She still had stitches on her elbow.

"I smell like shit," she said. "I need a shower."

I cracked open a beer from the mini-fridge.

"Go ahead and take one."

She went into the bathroom and I heard the water running. I sat alone on the bed in my undershirt and boxers and turned on the TV. There was nothing in the news that I could find about an American Cash Initiative being robbed. Each place was going to have a different name. I had told Ita earlier, over breakfast, how each one looked different and had a different layout inside. I'd been to almost all of them. They hired desperate people and loaned to even more desperate people to keep up the facade of being a real business. Half the time, they'd send their own enforcers to intimidate people into paying. I used to show up in the early morning for the mid-afternoon and make 'cash drops.' I wonder what they thought of a guy in a Pontiac Fiero or a Toyota Tundra coming to make cash drops and pickups instead of an armored truck. I wonder what they thought every time they called 'corporate' and talked to a pushy guy with a Kharkiv accent. The safe was usually store-bought, something you'd find in any half-ass drug dealer's walk-in closet. I was pretty explicit with Ita when it came to the possibility of killing anyone behind the counter. The people that worked there were just people. Sure, they might've had an idea that it wasn't legit, but weren't all title loan companies just mafias anyway? Those people had kids and rent to pay and worries. It wasn't fair to kill'em. I wasn't in this to kill anyone innocent, whatever that means. She seemed insulted that I felt the need to tell her that.

"So far, you're the only one here who's killed anybody," she said. "If someone has the balls to aim a gun at me, I'm gonna assume they're more than just an employee and I'm gonna drop'em."

"What if they're just some redneck with a hero complex?" She shrugged.

I took a swig of beer and walked to the bathroom door. It was unlocked. The room was filled with steam. Her body was a blur behind the textured glass. She rubbed herself with a bar of soap, lathering it in her hands beneath the trickle of mountain water. I sat down on the closed toilet and drank beer while I watched her shower.

"Are you my new captor?" she said. "I can't shower alone anymore?"

I finished the beer and tossed the can into the tissue bin.

"Why do you hate me so much?" I said. "We used to talk. We used to kiss."

"Please, leave me alone."

I walked out and lit a cigarette and kept watching TV. She came out wrapped in a towel and sat down beside me on the bed and put her arm around me.

"I don't hate you," she said.

"Seems like it."

"I don't. You saved my life."

"You don't owe me," I said.

"But it feels like I do. And that's what I hate," she said. "I hate myself, but I want to do something for myself."

She traced her scars with her fingers.

I placed my hand on the slashes down her wrists.

"I've never made a single decision on my own," she said. "I can't even kill myself without you saving me. You're the one who comes up with everything."

"You don't want to do this? You don't want any of this?"

"No," she said. "I want this. I just don't...I don't know what I'm trying to say."

I knew what she was trying to say, but I didn't know how to say it either. Looking at me reminded her of everything she'd been through. But when I looked at her, she only reminded me of the good times, the parts in-between the torture.

"I don't want you to see bad things when you see me," I finally said.

"Basil, I can't help it."

10

We split up the next day. She said she'd get a car herself and I took the Palio. We divided everything fifty-fifty: the money, the guns, the stops on the map. The mission was still on. She told me if we came out alive by October, she'd meet me at a parking lot on the Blue Ridge Parkway. I spent the next month driving through North and South Carolina, hitting title loan stores. I spent nights drinking hard and smoking crack in front of the TV news and reruns of Family Guy and The Simpsons. The police weren't catching on. I figured the Chechens were trying their best to keep it quiet. We were attracting a different kind of heat. I sat there on the cheap hotel floors wired out of my skull and fantasizing about the top brass coming down on Piotyr for the lost cash. Despite getting high and drunk every night, I did most of the robberies sober. I was scarier that way. I kept the same MO. There are only so many ways you can pull off a stickup. I put the pistol in the clerk's face and demanded to see the manager. The manager came out and I had everyone follow him like a conga line to the safe. The way they did it in the movies was never a good idea. They'd have everyone get on the ground with their hands flat and the robber would follow the manager to the safe. You don't want to isolate people. That's when they find opportunities to trip alarms, call the police, text 911, pull guns...You keep everyone together. You don't isolate or focus on one person. Even when the safe was just some little rinky-dink box any shotgun could blast apart, you give everyone a task, you make everyone complicit, which was easy since there were usually three people max. You yell at them constantly, a mix of insults and orders. Keep their brains racing. Don't let them calm down. Don't let them deduce anything. You rush them and you're gone. One person opens the safe and the other fills the bag with money. If there isn't a task to do, make one up. I made a girl sing once. She sang off-key while her eyes filled with tears. I should feel bad about it, but I don't.

I didn't know how Ita did hers, maybe the same. It was hard to tell with almost no news coverage. She asked me to let her go. I cried alone for days. My chest physically hurt when she left. I couldn't explain it. She told me that she still cared about me. She told me she cherished what I had done for her. But she needed this. It was the first time in her life she'd ever been on her own.

I rolled into the South Carolina capital city and got a room at a place called the Marlboro Inn close to the highway exit. The sign was a picture of a yellow apple with the rotten part cut out. I got a bottom-floor room facing the Fiat in the parking lot. I had a pretty good disguise. My shaved head had grown back and I colored it gray and white from a bottle to look older. I did the same for my mustache and soul patch. I wore Hawaiian shirts with long johns underneath and khaki pants. I told people I was a jazz musician. I even had a saxophone and a sax case I bought from a pawn shop. That's why I had to pay for the room in busking cash. As long as the hotel was dank enough, no one gave a shit. The Marlboro Inn was that kind of place. Fifty bucks a night. Jesus. Good God fuck. I picked up a six-pack at the gas station down the road and drove around drinking and driving, looking for a place to buy some crack. I steered clear of the white parts of town. All they'd have is meth, and I wasn't a tweaker. Meth was a poor man's twelve-hour high. That's how you stretched your dollar. Closeted gay men also liked it. I remember those BDSM parties when six or seven country lawyers used to pound me like a piece of meat strapped to a butcher's block in the center of the room, everyone taking hits off the glass bubbler full of ice. I liked the immediacy of a little coke. Crack didn't last long. Quick and easy. It was the cellphone game of hard drugs.

I drove all over the city and couldn't find anyone who would sell to me. Columbia was fresh out of crack. I went to the pharmacy and bought a box of Coricidin and swallowed the whole thing with beer on my way back to the hotel. I got super lucky. That night, I managed to evade every cop on the street and parked right in front of my room at the Marlboro Inn before I passed out onto the steering wheel.

I woke up with a red mark on my forehead from the wheel. Birds were chirping. The parking lot was nearly empty. I started the car and drove to a breakfast spot where I could drink enough coffee to force my body into wakefulness. I sat there in the booth for hours, eating an omelet drenched in Tabasco sauce, watching the sun rise over the church steeple from my corner window.

I dried out for a day before I robbed the next spot. The place was called AmeriCash Title Advance Lending Partners. It was interesting to see how many variations of the same idea they could come up with. I used the black 9mm. It looked the most intimidating. I wore a scary Halloween mask with a cowboy hat and gray sweats. There were two clerks behind the front desk. I rushed them and stuck the pistol in their faces as I crawled across the threshold. I screamed at them for the manager. They said he was out to lunch. I already had the front door locked, so I took them to the back and asked them to open the safe. They didn't pretend not to know the combo. The taller girl had it opened and I forced the other to hold a Panda Express bag open while she shoveled the money inside. I grabbed the money and locked the girls in the back room. I walked toward the door and saw the manager heading up the parking lot with a bucket of KFC in his arms. He stopped dead when he saw me. I showed him the gun and he turned back to his car.

I cut around the vine-covered brick wall to my car and jumped inside and sped through a narrow residential road. I pulled onto the boulevard as I ripped my hat and mask off. I took the gray sweatshirt off at a red light and donned some shades. I drove onto the highway exit and turned on the radio. That's when I noticed the manager in his Dodge Charger behind me. I merged in front of a tractor trailer and saw him accelerate in my rearview mirror.

"Ah, shit," I said to myself, gritting my teeth.

I gunned it through a procession of slow Cadillacs once I saw the first exit to a country road. I wandered through the foliage-dense road. I could see the Charger take the same exit over the bend. I came to a circle around a small lake. There was a goat farm in the distance. I took my chances and parked the Fiat in the empty lot near the fishing dock. I ducked low and ran across the road to the willow tree and waited. The Charger pulled up the lot. He was looking around for me. I didn't wait for him to get out of the car and opened fire with the Beretta. The windshield shattered. I could hear the startled goats bleating. The Charger drifted into a parking sign and stopped. I approached and opened the driver's side door. The manager slopped out onto the ground once I cut the seatbelt with my buck knife. He was still breathing. Blood poured out of his ruptured throat and mouth. I stood there and watched him drown and then I took the bucket of chicken and left.

11

used to sit up at night and wonder if someone was waiting for me in those thousands of motel parking lots with a gun. I'd become a ghost and I could haunt the room. I was watching an old British movie one night about a fancy hotel in London or somewhere like that with a cursed room where you dream the dream of the last person to sleep there. Even though I was drunk and numb with ENT-grade cocaine, I knew the premise didn't make any sense. Wouldn't everyone just have the same dream?

After a few months of terror and fear and dreams about them killing Ita and finding a way to send me pictures of her severed head, the dark hand of the Son's of Grozny, and the remnants of the Arkan mob found a way to get in touch with me. Someone had left a burner phone at each of the remaining title loan locations. The employees were told to give it to me if I robbed the place. Crazy.

I only took one in case Ita might have too. I pulled it apart in the car after my next robbery to see if they had a tracking device inside. Then I realized a phone *was* a tracking device nowadays. I drove to a ravine behind an industrial park and called the only contact number.

The phone rang.

"Da?"

"Ya Shaver."

"Mr. Shaver," he said, switching to an American accent. "Very nice to get a call from you. Thank you for using the phones. I understand you used to work for Piotyr Kamineski."

"Work? I don't know about that. I used to be his property. Where is he?"

"A significant loss of Obshchak on his part isn't acceptable. That's pretty much his whole position made useless. He was sent back to Grozny to take care of his mother."

Obshchak means gang-related funds. Going back to Grozny to take care of your mother meant you were dead.

"Grozny is looking for me?"

"I'm not Grozny, Mr. Shaver. Can I call you Basil?"

"Sure."

"I'm like you Basil. I'm a thief."

These guys talk in code half the time. It sounds congenial enough, but it's always a threat. Whoever I was talking to just now pulled rank on me. Telling me Grozny wasn't involved was his way of telling me that the Bratva, the Russian Mafia, was coming after me now. Then he said he was a thief. A thief, or a *vor*, is the highest-ranking boss in the organization. I may as well have been talking to the devil himself. This guy had an American accent which meant he probably grew up in the U.S. and almost no one from the new country gets to become a boss. I couldn't imagine what this guy had done to get where he was.

"Knowing where you come from, Basil," he said. "I'm pretty impressed. We don't let products usually start in the organization. One of the reasons why Piotyr had to go back to Grozny. But seeing how you've managed to hit this many places in this amount of time. You got some balls, and skills too. I'll tell you what. You've probably spent a good bit of the money. No worries. Just bring us back the lion's share and we'll hire you. A thief recognizes a thief. How'd you like to work for us?"

"Sounds too good to be true."

"I suppose it does. But it's better than any alternative. Who am I helping if I just kill you? We want our money and I'm sure you want another shot. This is it, kid."

"What about Ita?"

"The girl? She'll have to go back to Mexico to take care of her mother."

I was careful not to tell him we had split up. I figured she hadn't called them first.

"So that's it?"

"That's it. I give you my word on this," he said. "Understand that this is the extent of my compassion."

"Then I guess I'll see you in hell."

"You won't see me. But you'll be seeing someone."

I threw the cellphone into the ravine.

12

The Russian was right about how much money I had spent. What he didn't know about was all the money I had burned and tossed over highway bridges. I took and used as much as I needed but I couldn't haul around that much hard cash anyway. The point was to destroy them, to bleed them out. If the Russians had gotten involved, we were winning. I felt strangely empty knowing they had already killed Piotyr. I signed my death warrant when I refused their offer. It could have been a setup anyway. Who knows? I was wanted by someone worse than the cops now. The Russian Mafia had all kinds of unholy connections. They'd send a tracker after us, someone with a face like your next-door neighbor and a valid I.D. who speaks English like a little-league coach, someone you don't see in a crowd, a soldier with the emotional depth of a water moccasin.

I went to a little shop and bought a new burner phone to get in touch with Ita. It was the first time I talked to her in months. She sounded calm, or was it detached? I couldn't tell. I told her we had to meet. I told her about the Russians, about Piotyr. I drove to rural North Carolina the next day. I listened to Judas Priest and some other old-school rock music on the radio as I drove, sipping coffee, chain smoking cigarettes. I stopped at two rest stops along the way to throw up. I wasn't even hungover. My hands shook as I gripped the steering wheel. I kept thinking about what she would look like. My heart pounded. I can only imagine what I had done to it while binging on cocaine all the time. Fall had begun and the leaves were starting to turn once I reached the mountains. It was getting close to the evening when I pulled the Palio into that secluded lot on the parkway but the days were still long and warm like the summer. I sat on the hood of the small car and smoked. The lot sat on the edge of a giant cliff. There was a lookout on the plateau further off toward the treeline which had quarter telescopes and a safety railing. Tourists and hikers could see an endless expanse of brickle treetops. Vultures circled over a dead animal somewhere, peppering the blank sky like ants on a countertop. The cliff by the parking lot wasn't cordoned off by any safety bar or gate and I wondered how many drunk rednecks had driven over the edge. I waited for an hour, panicking in silence. A black, 1967 Imperial reached the hill and pulled into the lot among the pines and oak trees like a funeral hearse. The engine sounded like an Alligator's morning bellow, chugging as it idled in the distant parking space. I stood up and walked toward her. Ita got out and pulled a gun on me.

"Lift up your shirt," she said.

I lifted my shirt.

"You got a piece?"

I showed her the revolver.

"Why do you like that thing?"

"It's simple," I said. "I don't like those automatics. I worried they're gonna jam or go off."

"Toss it."

I reached into my pants and threw the gun into the grass.

She looked different. She had cut her hair a little shorter and dyed it a dark, natural red, almost auburn like some of the leaves. She wore a black Northface jacket with cargo pants and hiking boots. I noticed a fresh neck tattoo: the Mexican eagle holding a rattlesnake in its talons.

"You look different. I like it."

"You look old," she said.

"It's my disguise," I said. "It's dye."

I caught a look at her nails. They had been manicured.

"Oh, yeah, I forgot I gave you the nail salon."

"That big Romanian guy, all those Asian girls working off their trip."

"Yeah, Nico. I used to deal with him. He's dead?"

"No," she said as she put away her pistol. "But I rearranged his face for him."

"Good."

"You don't think it's strange the cops aren't after us?"

"They're not reporting the robberies. If they report it, what are they going to say? There's all kinds of dirty money they have to account for, books that don't exist."

She rolled her eyes.

"Maybe they think too highly of the state police. I was watching TV last night and I got an idea. Wasn't much of an idea. Just thought about it for a second, you know."

"Yeah?"

"We've crossed state lines, you know. What if we went to the FBI? Gave them names. You know. We could go into witness protection."

"Who would we give them? Everyone we had on them is dead. They already know half of what we know. I've already killed nine people. It's too late. No, we hand ourselves over and we're going to prison. Nothing would happen to the organization they couldn't walk away from. How about you? You killed anybody yet?"

She nodded.

"Yeah."

"I don't think it's a good idea."

"You can just tell me I'm stupid for saying it."

"You're not stupid, Ita."

"Don't...don't do that."

"What?"

"That thing you do. Don't do that."

I stopped for a moment and looked at the ground.

"They're sending someone aren't they?" she said.

"Yeah."

"A Russian?"

"No, a *vor* won't get his hands dirty. He'll send someone else."

"Someone like us."

I hadn't thought about it. It was possible.

"Do you think that's how their soldiers start out, getting fucked?"

"It's how we started," I said. "Can I ask you how you are?"

She sighed.

"Let's get out of here. I don't want to stand around too long."

"Can I get my gun?" I said.

"I'll get it."

"Which car do we take?"

"Yours."

"You drive yours off the cliff there?" I said.

"What? No. The authorities will be looking for it then."

She walked to the Imperial and lifted the hood.

"Park rangers will think it's broken down. Out here, it might sit for five or six days before they tow it."

"I guess I just wanted to see a car go over the side there."

She smiled and grabbed my pistol. She made me drive after checking the trunk and the cramped backseat of the Fiat and her grip on the butt of the gun for the first mile. After that, something shifted in her and she calmed down. I didn't try to figure out what she was thinking and I didn't talk either. I just kept my mouth shut and drove. I don't know how she felt but I didn't feel the same way about her. I didn't feel like it would matter if she walked away forever. I wouldn't hold it against her but I was glad to be with her. It felt like we were different people now. I guess we were.

When it got dark. I had a hard time on the mountain roads. The trees were so thick around us. You couldn't see the moon. The headlights were weak. I didn't like not being able to see. The silence was starting to hum in my ear. I can't explain it. I felt strange that night like we were already dead. If you kept digging past my casket, you'd find the trees and the road at night, a sovereign dream, blank stares from an unknown creature whose eyes you cannot see. I half expected to see a hitchhiker thumbing us down at the opposite end of the steel road barrier, but the shadow figure never showed up. Ita asked me if I was hungry. I was starved. There weren't any places to eat on the backroads. I pulled onto the main highway and eventually found a 24-hour gas station. We got out and I swiped the prepaid Visa card and pumped gas. Some night birds squawked overhead. The pale clerk looked at us like he'd been waiting there his whole life. I tried not to make eye contact. He seemed preoccupied with Ita as she loitered around the little store. The moon was a solid hue, the dull color of beaver teeth. I locked the doors to the little Brazilian-made car and walked into the store after Ita. It was like stepping inside of a meat locker. Nothing was hot. Nothing was fresh. All the food they had was crushed inside pull-tab cans and crystalized with so much sodium you could have smoked it in a crack pipe. I grabbed a fruity drink from the cooler and watched Ita dump a few bags of pork rinds on the counter in front of the clerk. There was a map behind him pinned to the wall with thumbtacks. It wasn't a functional map. It looked old like something you might see in a museum with ornate calligraphy and faded drawings of mountains and trees and deer. I was so tired. My knee was sore from shifting to the break every three seconds down the mountain. Ita got the drink and a stale pack of cigarettes. I asked her to drive

"Let's just stop somewhere and sleep."

"Did you see a motel on the exit sign?"

"We'll find one," she said.

We found some meth lodge close to the stateline with a lobby that smelled like juniper and chlorine. The room was crowded with musty furniture and the dark, machine-press, polyester rug was worn so thin around the perimeter of the bed that you could see the concrete floor underneath. The cinder blocks of the back wall were painted over directly with a cheap bucket of eggshell white. I almost thought I could taste the dust on the ceiling pipes. And there she was again beside me in the same bed like we were family. She had stripped down to her functional gray bra and loose panties. I read the healed-over scars on her body in the frantic glimmer of the television set. It was like old times, I suppose.

"I think I love you," I said.

"I don't have an answer for you."

"It's not a question."

"Everything you say to me is a question," she said. "I don't know what it is I can give you. I'd give my body but it's broken."

"It's not broken."

"It is," she said.

"My insides are probably mush by now. I'll have a heart attack before I'm old."

"It's not the same, Basil."

"I think you're beautiful," I said and kissed her.

She leaned into the kiss and grabbed my shoulder and then she bit my lip and let it slingshot back to my lower teeth. She still had that deep sadness behind her eyes I used to notice every time I saw her dance. The word 'slave' didn't look the same in her arm. The healed tissue bled the 'v' and the 'e' together.

"Don't look at that," she said. "I talked to a tattoo artist about covering it up."

"Same guy, that did the thing on your neck?"

"No."

"I like it."

"It's an identifying mark. I have to cover it up when I rob the spots."

"Do you still speak Spanish?"

"Of course, I do. It's my first language."

"Where did you get that old gangster car?"

"I bought it off another chop shop."

"I wish I knew how to work on cars. That'd be a good job."

"You and I weren't meant for anything besides this."

"Robbery and getting fucked?"

"Being garbage."

"You think we're garbage?" I said.

"I think you're stalling. Are you afraid to fuck me?"

"Maybe a little bit."

"Why?"

"I've never fucked before."

"What?"

"That's not what I mean," I said. "I've been fucked. I've gotten fucked a thousand times. Mostly by men. But I've never actively fucked anyone."

"What you're describing is rape," she said. "And rape isn't fucking. I read that somewhere."

"Was it always rape? Sometimes I'd just lay back and take it until my ass was bleeding on the couch or the bed or whatever. Senators with saggy chins and pot bellies holding me down until I couldn't breathe. Other times, they wanted to pretend I was their boyfriend. They'd kiss me and make me eat chocolates with them and suck my dick as much as I had to suck theirs. I couldn't say I didn't like it."

"You only liked it because they weren't beating the shit out of you at the time. I was the same way. We never had a choice one way or the other and that's what still makes it rape."

"You're right," I said. "Maybe that's it. Maybe I've never done it because I wanted to, not really...at least. I don't know."

"We don't have to," she said. "There's nothing that says we have to."

"I just like being next to you," I said, wrapping my arms around her midsection, listening to her heartbeat. "Do I still remind you of everything terrible?"

"After I left," she said. "Those first few days were great. I was on my own for the first time in my life. Then everything started to remind me of Piotyr and Oksana again. I couldn't get away from it. So it isn't just you."

I didn't know what to say next.

She laughed a little.

"What?"

"You said you love me but you're afraid to fuck me."

"Is that funny?"

"I don't know."

"Have you healed," I said, placing my hand on the front of her panties.

"Pretty much."

"Can you still feel?"

"Yeah, she didn't cut it off. She just...well...you saw it."

I stuck my hand inside her and moved up and down. She exhaled and closed her eyes as I caressed her. I pinched some of the damaged skin, lightly, between my knuckles and started stroking the light indentation of the shaft above her clit. I knew what to do because I had done it once or twice before and I had seen it done a thousand times. The scarred hood exposed its raw interior. She raised her legs and took off her panties while I pulled her breasts out of her bra. She reached behind and unstrapped it and tossed it on the floor. I took my clothes off. She licked her thumb and circled the tip of my dick. It got even harder. She worked the tip like a clit and then she grabbed the base and started tugging upward. A little clear liquid dribbled out onto the sheets.

"You like it gentle," she said.

"Do you?"

She shrugged.

"I want to forget I'm here. You don't have a condom do you?"

"I don't."

"I haven't had birth control since we left Beaufort. We can't bring a kid into this."

"No," I said.

She bunched the pillows and sheets at the top of the bed to support herself. I kissed her back. She reached between her legs and wetted her hand. I watched and kissed the backs of her thighs. She shifted her arm around awkwardly and, with her elbow bent, rested her palm on her tailbone, letting the moisture from her fingers run down the tender portions of her skin. I spat. She mixed my saliva with the fluid from her fingertips around the opening. I spat again and kept rubbing until I could force my way through. She sighed and winced. I asked if she was okay and she told me to keep going. I pushed in and out. She told me I was too afraid. I said I wasn't afraid. Her knuckles tightened as she gripped the sheets. I did everything she said. She burst into tears and told me not to stop, even if I was afraid. I said I wasn't afraid. I leaned over her. She shook beneath me. I told her I wasn't afraid.

13

I came inside her and then tried to rub her clit again until orgasm. She replaced my hand with her own and finished. The tip of my prick was covered in reddish-brown shit. My cum ran down from between her ass cheeks to her leg as she walked to the bathroom. I followed. We cleaned off in the shower together and put on our old clothes and got back in bed. I asked her why she cried so much when I fucked her.

"I like crying," she said. "I'm tired of holding it all in. The other girls used to put a pillow over your face if they caught you crying in the middle of the night."

"Guess you're making up for the lost time."

She turned off the TV.

I fell asleep.

We got up early the next day and drove east toward the coast. The terrain flattened out as we drove through what seemed like acres of deserted farmland.

"Want to stop at a barbecue place?" I said.

"Stop at a gas station and buy some condoms, make sure they're not expired."

It took a long time until we found a gas station. I bought a few condoms and some coffee. We looked for a secluded spot off the highway. I cut through the grass median since we were the only car on the road for miles and went down a small backroad until we saw a derelict pharmacy building. I parked in the back between the vine-covered brick and the pine trees. I sat on the hood of the Fiat and rolled down my pants to put on the first condom. She left her pants and underwear in the car and climbed on top. I could still feel her inner warmth through the latex. She squatted over me and started to pump. I helped her as much as I could, pushing up with my lower body. She didn't cry this time. She stayed quiet. She looked determined, focused like an athlete. Her pussy juice dripped down my cock and puddled and streaked across my pelvis. I didn't cum. She did. I was glad for her. I jacked off to finish and threw the dripping, full rubber into the woods. We got back into the car and drove for another hour before Ita spotted a little Mexican restaurant in a lonely strip mall. We went inside still smelling like sex and drank tall glasses of icewater and ate tortilla chips with hot salsa. The booths were made of fake leather, the backs of which towered over our heads. There was a small stereo on the bartop beneath the hanging margarita glasses playing a sad ranchera which barely masked the harsh noise of the kitchen.

I asked Ita what the song meant. She said she didn't know. It was something about being lost in the plains, the stare of a wolf on a cliff, a broken heart, the ghost of a drowned boy pulling the singer into a river...She was only translating the parts she could hear as the song carried on. They brought us our food which tasted okay. There was a lot of cinnamon in the sauce. I felt full and sluggish. I was out of coke and the waitress didn't look like the holding type. I asked Ita if she had any uppers. She showed me a little bag of ice. I didn't like meth but we had nothing else. We tipped the waitress $40 and took turns going to the bathroom to do rails. I was wired. My heart raced. Ita looked used to it, comfortable even. The Chechens used to give the strippers in the club meth to keep them from having to sleep and eat everyday. My hands shook like I had nerve damage whenever I took amphetamines. We left the restaurant and, as we walked to the car, Ita grabbed the crotch of my jeans. She pointed to a park bench facing the vacant lot between two empty storefronts.

"You still have those condoms on you?"

"You want to fuck outside? Right here?"

She walked toward the bench, letting me choose to follow her or not.

I was jittery, manic with the growing effect of the meth. I need to do something intense and repetitive. I made sure I had the condoms in my jean pocket and followed her to the bench. She knelt on all fours across the graffitied bench and pulled down her pants. I unzipped and rolled on the condom. We fucked harder this time; less intimacy and more energy. I blew my breath forward like a jogger scaling a hill. Ita was breathing loud enough for me to hear her. We pushed against each other. She looked back at me, smiling as she grasped the edge of the dirty seat. I felt everything inside her tighten She started screaming, yelling at me to fuck her. I kept going. I didn't even check to see if anyone could see us. It felt like we were the only people on earth. I don't know if it was my own insanity or the meth-induced tunnel vision. It crossed my mind that this is what my rapists over the years must have felt like...somewhat...maybe. But it wasn't out of anger. It was joy, blind, unhinged joy; both of us working toward the same endgame. I was swollen with blood. I looked down and saw the pink and purple parts inside of her turn red with friction. The metal sides of the bench began to separate from the ground. She arched her back and spread her legs wider. Her pelvis and stomach jiggled with a healthy layer of brand new fat cushioning her from my skeletal midsection. I rested my trembling hands on her waist and felt the heat coming off her. She pushed back, taking in my entire cock. I stopped and held her in silence. She grabbed my hand and pulled it around to her crotch as she lifted herself upright on her bare knees. I was still inside her as she used my forefinger to masturbate, guiding me with her hand. Her body spasmed. I thought I could feel my heartbeat inside my cock as it throbbed. Her stomach quivered and her hips shook as she let out an audible sigh. A red pickup truck drove past us. The owner of the Mexican restaurant stepped out from the back of the building annex to yell at us. He screamed at the top of his lungs and told us he had called the police. We both finished cumming in front of him. Milky fluid dribbled from between her legs as I pulled out and tore off the condom. He warned us to leave again. I put on my pants in a hurry. With a defiant smile on her face, Ita stayed where she was and started pissing. Her clear stream of urine showered the park bench.

"You like this," she said. "Is this what you like?"

The owner went silent as if he were just punched in the gut.

She kept touching her exerted body as she finished pissing.

"Is this what you do to your wife or to girls because your wife won't let you? Have you ever bought a girl to fuck before?"

The man stared at her bare, red vagina for a moment, turned around, and walked away.

"I'm going to call the police," he repeated under his breath.

14

I stood on the beach at low tide. The sand felt tough under my bare feet like a ridge of solid concrete beneath a layer of hardened grit. Ita walked down through the sticky muck to the edge of the water where the short waves arched and broke and condensed the weightless clusters of seafoam across the shoreline. The pier at the opposite end of the inlet looked like a rig in the darkness and the diminished ocean like a black lake of excess crude seeping from the earth. I thought of sharks circling out past the buoy toward the barrier islands. One of the motel brochures said there were still wild pygmy horses living on the scattered peninsulas and disappearing islands. I wondered if horses slept at night.

The side of Ita's face burned through the shadow as she turned and cupped the flame to light her cigarette. I could feel the sand biting at my ankles in the wind. The small light died as she took her thumb off the Bic.

I walked down the strand and sat on the beached log of driftwood. The outline of Ita's hair against the open sky and oil-colored water tangled in the breeze. She walked back up to our shoes and socks with the red ember between her fingers and sat down beside me on the log. We both saw another light coming toward us: a handheld flashlight beam sweeping from one end near the dunes and then back down to the water.

"Somebody walking?" she said.

"Maybe. Probably."

I reached into my jacket and grabbed the handle of the snub-nose revolver. Ita flicked the butt across the sand. The half-cigarette was swept away in the violent wind with its loose, glowing embers scattering like fireflies. The figure with the flashlight moved closer. I couldn't make out a face behind the light but the shadow's frame looked male. I took the revolver out of my jacket and hid it behind my thigh with my finger flat on the trigger guard. I could hear Ita reaching for her compact Sig Sauer. The flashlight's glare stopped moving from side to side and stayed on the rigid course as the stranger inched toward us. It was about 10-feet away when the light shut off. I could hear an island coyote yap from the dunes. The figure stopped dead and stood there like a mannequin in the dark. I heard an old man's voice call out to us.

"Is anyone there?"

"Yeah," Ita said.

"Did you hear that coyote?"

"Is that what that was?" she said.

"Yeah, they're everywhere is what they say now. Hey, where are you?"

She didn't say anything.

"Only reason I ask is 'cause I don't want to bother you with my flashlight but it's the only way I can see where I'm going."

"Go ahead."

His light switched on as I heard what sounded like a car backfiring, a muffled crack. The sand kicked up beside me. Ita extended her arm and fired back. I saw the muzzle flash of the Sig. The little pistol sounded like thunder crashing over the beach. I aimed as best I could and shot at the ghost. His silhouette fell back. A bullet pierced the flashlight lens. I heard a hollow whistle as the plastic, the glass, and the thin aluminum snapped all at once.

We approached the man sprawled out across the sand. Black blood leaked from his ruptured gut. He was thin and he wasn't an old man. The voice could have been fake. Ita stood above him and held her pistol over his face. He reached up to shield himself. The bullet passed through the gaps in his fingers, collapsing his eye socket. The back of his skull split open.

"He had a silencer," she said, pointing to the stray Glock with a long black cylinder affixed to the barrel.

We didn't see how much blood had sprayed onto our clothes until we were inside the car, heading back to the motel. We took turns showering and watching the parking lot through the closed blinds. We parked the car in the alley behind an oyster bar. Once Ita had changed, she put the bloody clothes in a black garbage bag and stashed them under the mattress. We had nothing to eat. I was too scared to leave the room. The little coastal town seemed abandoned anyway. I sat down on the floor with my back to the bed.

"How long do you think he tailed us for?" Ita said.

I looked up at her.

"How did he find us in the first place? Did you take a phone from one of the spots? Anything they can track us with?"

She shook her head.

"We could have tortured it out of him if you hadn't killed him so quick."

She scowled at me.

"Maybe, he followed the local TV. Police called after couple fucks outside in public."

"I doubt it," she said. "Didn't you say they're going to find us one way or the other? You need to stop being a coward."

I watched her as she took the new shotgun from its case. She tore open a box of shells and started forcing them into the loading port.

"What are you doing?"

She ignored my question.

"You're acting like you didn't come up with this thing. Did you seriously think we'd live on the run and fuck each other like animals for the rest of time? They have eyes everywhere. If they want us, they'll find us. The fun is over."

"I don't think that," I said.

"You're acting like it."

"I'm just trying to figure out how he found us on the beach."

A pair of headlights lit up the blinds behind me. The high beams shined through the gaps in the yellowing plastic like stadium flood lights. I grabbed the loaded 1911 off the side table and crouched behind the bed next to Ita. She carefully racked the shotgun. I could hear an engine running beyond the narrow threshold. A heavy car door slammed. Shoes scraped against the sidewalk. Ita rested the stock against her shoulder, propping her elbows across the bedspread. I aimed the silver pistol, clutching the carbon-fiber grip.

Silence.

The person on the other side steered clear of the window. All I could see was the intense light. Ita let out a short breath as she looped her finger over the trigger.

I swallowed.

A bullet struck the motel-room door. Ita returned fire with the buckshot. To our surprise, the door didn't splinter. It was made of metal, compressed aluminum which caught the flattened pellets. The shooter fired a few more rounds, warping the door. He moved in front of the window. I could see his shadow and took my chance, firing the entire magazine. The glass shattered. The .45 ACP sailed through the window and echoed as it struck the vehicle outside. The light receded as the car reversed, its tires screeching. Ita jumped over the bed and ripped the last dangling pieces of the blinds from the window frame. The wind bellowed into the room. The gunman, dressed in a dark hoodie, hobbled feebly after a black van with six bullet holes in the windshield. A trail of blood traced his path from the sidewalk to the center of the parking lot. The van abandoned him, speeding down the road. Ita took her shot. The blast knocked him flat on his face. His body twitched and then stopped. There were sirens already howling in the distance.

"Let's go," she said.

15

There are bibles in all motel rooms. I think that's strange. It doesn't make any sense to me. I guess it's extra joint paper at best because I don't think a thick, unapproachable book like the King James Bible offers any suicidal person comfort in their feverish, manic state, cutting themselves or fiending on smack...I just...who the fuck can read that book? I haven't been to school since the seventh grade but I know how to read and I know how people are and I can't imagine they're compelled by this book, at least not when they're ready to swallow their gun. It's an "old language" as they say. Who uses old language to talk someone down from a ledge? I think a dictionary would do just about the same amount of help in a motel room. I'm serious. To know the meaning of a word is a powerful thing. I guess I'm trying to sound deep. I don't have to try to sound smart. I know I'm smart. I'm just writing. I'm writing because there is nothing else to do. One of the palmettos near the entrance finally uprooted in the wind and knocked out a power line. The lights went out in the room and the TV set died. I'm writing this next to the window now to see what I'm doing. My hand is sore. I've been writing non-stop. These are my memories. There's nothing else to do.

The smoke from my cigarette pours into my eyes. The ash falls onto the pad and I wipe it away. It smudges like charcoal. The ashtray is full. There's a thin layer of tequila left in the bottle at my feet. Debris flies past the window. My knuckles are raw and pink. Yesterday, I tried to take a shower and the water turned brown. I've taken a sharp tactical blade and started hollowing out the bible from the bedside drawer. It's extremely difficult. When I'm done writing all of this down, I'll fold up those loose pages and set them inside the hollow book for safe keeping. I don't know what I'll do with it after that. Take it to a police station? A TV studio? A government building? I don't know. I'm just trying to get it all down.

I'm sitting here trying to remember what happened after that night. This is where my photo-perfect memories start to slip. Too much cocaine and meth. I remember burning the Fiat outside a tomato farm. I remember loading our things in a Chevy Geo we got by bribing a Mexican junkyard owner. We drove. We ate. We stopped somewhere in South Carolina and watched the news story about the murdered man at the motel on the TV above the bar. Ita said something about the cops coming after us now. I wasn't listening to her, not all the way at least. I was staring at the TV watching the news anchor talk. She was a small girl, younger than us, with red hair and a faded blue pantsuit. The motel looked different in the daylight. The destroyed window had a board of plywood covering it already and the parking lot was cordoned off by police tape. I kept watching. The police officers didn't have a comment for the network. They didn't connect the burning Palio to us.

They didn't even mention it. We drank in the corner dressed like a couple of tired day laborers as our new disguise to blend in with the rest of the lonely midnight alcoholics and pool-hall regulars (white Southern rednecks and Latinos alike in a strange comingling of groups that naturally hated each other). There was a weird-looking plastic Joshua tree in the corner next to a wooden cigar-shop Indian. I remember Piotyr taking me to a trailer park deep in the swamps once where he traded a couple of kilograms of coke with a native Edisto family who ran moonshine and brown smack. The plastic Joshua tree was out of place in the bar and strange to see in the lowcountry or the Peedee region. As far as I knew, it was a desert tree. I started to wonder if heading west was a good idea. Just run out into the desert and never be seen again. It was unlikely. It was getting late and Ita and I were slamming back the whiskey and beer hard enough to rack up an $80 tab in a place where the most expensive beer was six dollars. The bartender, a built-looking truckstop type, told us we drained his last bottle of Benchmark, so if we wanted to keep going we could pay for the good stuff (Wild Turkey Rye) or settle for Mellow Corn. I didn't want to know what that piss-yellow shit in the dusty bottle would taste like so we moved on.

I looked at the cigar shop Indian one last time and left. I don't know how we got home or what we did for the next two days or so. I can't imagine I did anything other than sleep and run through every awful mistake and crime I had ever committed in my short lifetime.

Ita was still cutting herself from time to time, especially when she drank but she wasn't trying to kill herself. There was a row of razorblade slices going down her left forearm she could hide in her jacket. We were sick from all that bottom-shelf whiskey and I'm sure if anyone wanted to walk into our motel room in the next few days they could have.

I kept thinking about the desert and the Indian caricature. My uncle, the only person who was ever kind to me, used to tell me stories about our family history. He didn't have any pictures or anything to back his stories and I am only now starting to wonder if he made them up. He told me about my grandfather getting lynched by the Kokomo chapter of the Indiana KKK and about the Indian Territory of the 1800s. His stories, if they were false, were incredibly detailed and I remember holding onto every word as a kid because no one else talked to me the way he did. He said my great-great-great-grandfather, his great-great-grandfather, was a Cherokee Freedman, a former slave who kept on living in the Indian territory. He said his name was Tsala Freeman. The name Tsala was not African. It was taken from 'Tsalagee' or 'Tsalaki' or 'Chalagee.' The Cherokee approximation of the English word 'Cherokee.' And since he was a former slave and then a freed man, that's the name he took. This mythical, faceless ancestor, Tsala, became a kind of childhood obsession of mine for a little while. The idea of a black man driving cattle across the sparse ranges of Oklahoma, speaking Indian, trading with Indians, and shooting them if they tried to stiff him. I had cowboy blood in my veins. Black cowboy blood. It was a nice dream. Or perhaps it was true and the gun I was holding was my birth-right. I stood up from the motel bed, still a little sick, and stared at myself, shirtless, in the mirror. I grabbed the silver, carbon-fiber grip, on the Colt 1911 that sat beside our toothbrushes and miniature tube of Crest and ejected the magazine. It slid out and landed upright on the counter. I pulled back the slide and let the chambered round, a fat, brass coated horse pill of a cartridge, fly out and roll around in the sink. The mechanisms of the pistol were amplified in the bathroom. I stared at myself in the dirty mirror and pointed the gun at the glass.

Tsala Freeman rode a mop-footed Ardennes through the mud on a black patch of charred earth where the lighting had set fires to the few trees along the lowlands. The pouring rain warped the brim of his hat and darkened the leather on his triangular satchel bag holding his '73 single-action pistol. His clothes stuck to his skin. The horse was stocky and unsuited for the long haul. He stole it off the Belgian who tried to ransack his camp. He shot the strange little man four times.

How do I know all this? How did I imagine it? I saw it. I smelled the mud. I felt the heat coming off the blackened lightning-struck trees! I saw everything. I saw the pistol and the horse, the endless hundred-year-old range within a state I had never been to before. I stared at myself in the mirror holding the automatic against the mirror. Two guns touch-ing. I smiled at my reflection. Tsala kept riding. I picked the cartridge out of the sink and set it in my mouth. I plucked another out of the magazine and set them both under my top lip like fangs. The horse whinnied. There was thunder in the distance. My bullet teeth dropped from my mouth as my grin widened. I pressed the empty pistol against my temple just to see what it looked like. Tsala took shelter under a rocky over-hang and rolled a cigarette of pipe leaf tobacco he bought off a Chickisaw agent and lit it with a weak flame from a French match. I could smell burning sugar, rubber, and sulfur before the clean scent of sun-dried tobacco leaves. I looked behind my shoulder in the reflection and saw smoke rise from the shower. I pulled away the curtain and found Ita in the tub with a cigarette burning and a fresh razor blade on the white edge amid specks of fresh blood. She was slicing her thigh and then pouring hand sanitizer into the cuts for the sting. I asked her what she was doing. She said she was relaxing and asked what I was doing. I put my bullet fangs back in and stuffed the pistol into my crotch.

"You're weird," she said.

I turned back to the mirror and grinned again. The cartridges dropped from my mouth like loose baby teeth.

When the rain stopped, Tsala Freeman kept riding. He had people after him. I knew it. And in his possession, besides his bedroll and gun and tobacco and matches, he had a worn copy of the Bible.

16

₽

17

There was one last stop on the map we hadn't robbed. We didn't dare touch it. The place was probably under 24-hour surveillance, with Russian gangsters waiting in a series of tinted-window Mercedes SUVs. Instead, we double-hit a few more places. Same employees. Same managers. The scores were about the same and instead of burning it or dropping it off the side of an overpass, we stashed it in the Geo.

It was getting harder to get a hotel room. Now and then we'd see a police sketch scotch-taped to the lobby window and the Crimestoppers hotline number. We'd circle the block and leave. Not all places cared, but our options were getting slimmer.

You might find this hard to believe, but we stopped doing hard drugs around this time. It wasn't a conscious decision. It just happened. It seemed like going out and buying it was too much of a risk. We sat up nights watching the windows, talking about the limited experiences of our lives. We talked about what we thought happened after we died.

"I know what I'd like to happen," I said.

"What you'd like to happen?"

"Yeah, like my fantasy."

"What's the point?"

I shrugged.

"It's better than what I actually think will happen."

"What do you think will happen?" she said.

"Nothing."

"You believe in nothing."

"Don't you?"

She didn't answer.

We heard a noise from the edge of the bushes. Our attention immediately turned to the far window of the room. It was just a group of college students laughing as they tossed beer bottles into the sticker bushes on the end of the sidewalk.

"Do you think normal people know anything about people like us? Or do they care?"

"I don't think they know," I said.

"Really? You don't think they know?"

I shook my head.

"When I used to do private parties, mostly for other members of the gang. Every once in a while other Americans and even Mexicans would book me and a few other girls for a night. In those hotel rooms, there used to be bars of soap in the bathrooms with phone numbers on them. You were supposed to call and they would help you, you know. It was like some kind of women's organization. Oksana found that soap wrapper folded up in a girl's bra once. They beat her so fucking bad."

"I know. I was there," I said.

"You were?"

"Yeah, you don't remember?"

"I remember her screaming," she said. "I remember this one time a group of women was driving around the neighborhood giving gift bags to girls on the stroll. They came into the club and gave us all these little green bags with gold-trimmed tissue paper. It had shampoo, lotion, toothbrushes, toothpaste, tampons, condoms, soap, perfume, and information cards with the same hotline number. Alosh let them give them to us and after they had left, he threw them away. He let some of us keep the tampons and lotions."

I pointed to the snub-nose.

"I killed Alosh with this gun."

"Yeah?"

"Yeah. He decked me the night I came to get you. We fought on the ground and I got this thing at just the right angle and I killed that motherfucker. Piotyr was gonna have him kill me."

"So it's Alosh's gun?"

"It's my gun now. Half these guns are the ones I stole from them that night."

"I can tell. They were dirty as shit," she said.

We had spent close to three thousand dollars on new guns and ammo and things Ita said would keep up the guns.

"You said you learned all about guns from talking to johns. Is that true?" I said.

"Sort of," she said. "I used to steal magazines. The easiest ones to steal were the gun magazines. I didn't care about guns. I just wanted something from the outside, you know? Like a lifeline. Sure, I talked to some of the johns. Some liked to talk. Some. But what did they have to say anyway? Yeah, I had a stack of gun magazines under my cot at the bordello. So what?

I bet you're glad I did because back in Ohio...remember? You couldn't shoot for dogshit."

"I know," I said.

We came to a little town close to the border of North Carolina called Rock Hill. There was a spot we meant to rob in the next town over. It was 10 o'clock at night and it was raining hard. We pulled into an EconoLodge but the police sketch was up in the window so we drove around looking for another shitty slum to crash in. Ita had a new burner with a touch screen and a few apps loaded onto it. She said there was supposed to be a motel on the other side of town past the university campus. I saw lightning in the distance. Streaks of icy blue light dropped down from the sky. We passed a police station as we followed the GPS.

"There's too much heat here," I said.

"Nothing's going on between here and North Carolina," she said. "This town's dead."

"Only because it's raining."

When we got to the other motel, the place was abandoned. The windows were boarded up. The lights were out.

"Shit."

"It was too close to the police station anyway."

I thought I could see someone staring back at us through a broken corner of a top-floor window.

There were probably homeless junkies inside. We kept driving as the storm got worse.

"You want to stop at a gas station or a drive-thru or something?"

The lightning flashed overhead. The wind and the rain seemed to move the dangling branches of the trees in slow motion.

"Yeah, see what's open at least," I said.

I turned the car around and drove along a narrow boulevard lined with willows shuddering in the storm. On the right, surrounded by a thicket of bamboo, stood a rectangular building with a glass front and glowing neon signs. Beyond that, we could see stainless steel tables and chairs, napkin dispensers, salt and pepper shakers, parmesan cheese and red-pepper flakes, a counter, and a conveyor belt oven. The sign read 'Rustys Pizza' with no apostrophe, open 24-hours. The parking lot was little more than a gravel plot amid the bamboo. I parked without asking Ita if she wanted pizza. She didn't complain. We ran through the rain and pushed through the glass door. The bell rang. We wiped our feet on the red mat near the counter. A tall man with a ponytail stepped out from the back. He had a red flannel shirt and a silver buckle cover on his belt. He sipped from a cup of coffee and stared past us at the bursts of lightning.

"Ooh, spooky," he said, gesturing toward the front. "Y'all here to get some good pizza or you just taking shelter from the storm, as Dylan would say?"

"Dylan?" Ita said.

"Bob Dylan. Ain't y'all got no culture. What are they teaching you up at that college?"

We didn't bother telling him we weren't students.

He asked us what kind of pie we wanted and we shrugged like idiots. He reached across the counter and unfolded the menu in front of us.

"What exactly are we looking for?"

We wasted his time going over the toppings before we chose a simple twelve-inch sausage pizza with thin crust and sat down. There was another man in the small restaurant. A

little Latino kid with flour all over his apron and a hairnet with
a cigarette behind his ear. He kneaded the dough and twirled
it in his hand, something I had only seen done on TV. The
man with the ponytail put on some music. I assumed he would
play some Bob Dylan, but I don't remember what it was that
he played.

I saw the clock tower from the college campus against the
clouds in the flash of light. The thunder almost shook the windows of the restaurant.

"Where do we go from here?" Ita said.

I shrugged.

"Keep driving or keep looking."

"Sleep in the car?"

"There's no room in that shit box," I said.

We sat in silence and ate pizza and drank Heineken. Ita
covered her slices in red pepper flakes. The storm passed but
the rain continued. A Jeep pulled up beside our car in the
gravel lot and a group of kids, probably college students, got
out and walked into the shop. They were picking up a stack of
six pizzas. A guy with a leather jacket and a beanie stared at Ita.

"You got rained out from the venue too?"

"What?"

"The concert," he said. "The one they canceled."

We both shook our heads.

The girl behind him nudged his shoulder, telling him to
leave us alone.

"Who was playing?"

"What?"

"At the concert, who was playing?"

"Everybody," another girl said. "All local bands."

The group paid for their pizzas and left.

Ita stared at me as if to ask why I had engaged them.

I just shrugged and took a sip of beer. Even I didn't know why.

The strange owner was back behind the counter sipping from his constantly full coffee cup. I could hear the Latino cook cleaning dishes in the back.

"How's that pizza treating y'all?"

"It's great," I said, feeling strange responding to anything other than animosity and suspicion.

"How y'all like the music?"

"Is this Bob Dylan?" Ita said.

He shook his head.

"No, this is Jim Croce. Another old-timer. Gets me through these long nights."

"Are you always open so late?"

"24-hours a day, 6 days a week."

"That sounds like a lot."

"It makes sense being so close to Winthrop."

"Winthrop?"

"The college. Y'all ain't from here?"

"No."

"Huh. You passing through or visiting?"

"Passing through."

I looked at Ita wondering why she was talking so much with the owner.

He set down his coffee.

"Say, y'all want to try something?"

"Sure," she said

"Wait here."

He went into the back and came out with two plates. Each had a cylinder-shaped pastry that smelled of cinnamon and brown sugar.

"Churros," Ita said. "I remember these."

"They're still a little cakey. We haven't gotten the recipe down just yet, so I figured I'd test it out on the out-of-town folks."

We ate the churros and finished our beer and got back in the car.

"Is that what normal life is like?" Ita said, turning toward me.

18

We spent the night in a parking lot beside a public park. The backseat was cramped and my knees ached in my dream. The pain woke me up just as the sun rose above the hill, shining through the droplet-covered windows. I did my best to stretch. Ita had slept the night in the passenger's seat, fully reclined. I nudged her shoulder. She swatted my hand away.

I crawled over the driver's seat and through the door. The air was cold and the leafy asphalt was wet and slick. I took a piss behind a public trashcan and watched the steam rise. I was halfway through zipping up when a police cruiser rounded the turn and slowed, blocking in the Geo. Its tires crushed the fallen acorns. The cop kept the cruiser idling as he got out.

"Good morning."

"Good morning," I said.

"We'd prefer you use the lavatory at the Welcome Center," he said.

"I'm sorry. It was an emergency."

"Is this your car?"

"It's my girlfriend's car."

"Is she in the car?"

"Yeah, that's her."

"Okay," he said, putting his hands on his hips. He looked young with his boyish face and military-style haircut, the kind where they shave the sides and let the top grow out. He seemed like he might have strange ideas that he kept mostly to himself. I couldn't say why. He asked me for an I.D. and my girlfriend's I.D. and the registration of the car and proof of insurance.

I said "Yeah, of course," and I shot him six times in the chest.

His Kevlar vest absorbed the impact.

Ita, startled awake by the gunshots, instinctively ducked below the engine before kicking open the passenger's door to see what I had done.

"He's not dead," I said.

We rushed him and got rid of his belt. Ita couldn't pry the gun out of the retention holster.

The kid gasped.

I searched for a body cam. He wasn't wearing one. I ripped off the shoulder mic and went around to pop the hatchback door. I took the guns out and set them in the backseat.

"What are you doing?"

"Making room," I said. "I don't want him to grab a gun."

"We're not taking him."

"Yeah, we are," I said.

Once the trunk was empty, I pulled a bottle of whiskey and started pouring it across the dashboard and interior of the cruiser.

"That doesn't work like bleach," she said.

"I know."

"Then why are you doing it?"

"Confusion."

I took the remainder of the bottle and tried to force it down the cop's throat. All he did was spit it up and choke. Ita leaned over and pistol-whipped him.

"We can't waste any more time," I said.

I took my empty gun and cracked his nose. The blood started flowing the instant the hot cylinder crashed into his septum, covering the spaces around his lips and chin like facial hair.

Ita pulled the steel handcuffs from the belt.

I pressed his wrists together for her.

"Behind his back," she said.

We got him cuffed and threw him into the back. The trunk lid was missing, exposing him to the world as we drove away.

"People can see him," she said.

"I know."

I stuck to the back roads, flanked on both sides by trees and cow pastures. The cop was yelling for help. I didn't bother telling him to shut up.

"We should have gagged him," Ita said.

I didn't say anything. I still wasn't sure what we were going to do.

His face appeared in the rearview mirror as he fought his way over the back seat.

Ita drew the yellow taser.

"Don't kill him," I said.

She pulled the trigger and the metallic probe shot into the white of his neck as the connecting wire unspooled. His muscles tensed. He clenched his teeth in pain and fell back. Ita waited a moment before pulling the wire back like a short fishing line and stuffed the taster into the glove box.

He went silent.

I could feel her eyes on me as I drove and turned briefly to take a quick look at the smirk on her face.

"What?"

"I just tased a cop," she said.

"That makes you feel good for some reason?"

"What's a cop ever done for you?"

"Nothing, I guess."

She put a cigarette in her mouth.

"I've seen cops on the take before," she said. "I don't have any empathy for this guy. Why did you take him?"

"He might know something."

"You want to interrogate him? About what? The cops already have a description. Now they know about the car because he probably called it in. What is he gonna tell us?"

I listened to her and kept glancing in the rearview to make sure he was still incapacitated.

"You know we're gonna have to kill him."

19

More than one local news station ran the story of the missing cop, playing and replaying the same pictures. There was one of him on duty, one of him outside at a family barbecue, and one of him posing for his police academy graduation. During a televised news conference, the town sheriff looked straight into the camera and told us that we would be found and we will be punished. One station filmed his cruiser on the secluded park road in the dead of night behind police tape with the door ajar as if supernatural forces had ripped him from the front seat. They kept playing the footage in the corner of the screen as they spoke. They had a description of a tall man with dark hair and a detailed description of the car but nothing on a female accomplice. We kept the TV on 24/7 and tilted the screen from where it sat on the dresser toward the bathroom where we kept the cop strapped to a chair inside the tub. Ita bought the cables and duct tape at Walmart and tied him herself. We had stripped him down to his socks and underwear and turned on the cold shower water if he made any noise. I had learned the trick at the bordello.

The motel faced a derelict church with a fenced-in basket-ball court overrun with weeds and kudzu. It was called The Algodon, which, according to Ita, was Spanish for cotton. The mossy roof and cracked stucco arches were covered in fallen pine needles and the doors to the rooms were covered in chipping blue paint. The box springs under the mattress sounded like a train pulling into the station when I sat down. On the first day, Ita went out with the car and came back with Hardee's cheeseburgers and malt liquor. It was dangerous taking the car out but she did it anyway. She did what she could to change the look, spray painting the hood and side doors dark black. She coated the rest in a silver sheen and stole a new license plate from a junkyard lot and just transferred the sticker.

I asked the cop if he was hungry and fed him half a burger. It was strange feeding him by hand. I let him sip my coke through the straw. There was already whiskey in it.

"You smoke?"

He nodded.

I put a cigarette between his lips and struck a cardboard match. He smoked it for a while and then spit it down into the tub. It fizzled in the cold water.

"Do you know what they do to cop killers?" he said.

"You can't intimidate me," I said. "You can try. But I doubt there's anything you can say to me that would bother me."

He spat.

"If they find me, I swear to God, I'll personally cut off your nuts."

I lit a cigarette for myself.

"What do the cops know about us?" I said.

"I'm gonna tie you both up to the back of my truck and drag you two to Mexico if I get a chance."

I sighed.

"You want to have a pissing contest? See which one of us can come up with the most fucked up shit? My own life will beat your imagination every goddamned time. While you were captain of the football team and going to prom at the Double Tree, I was upstairs in room 309 with my wrists tied to bedposts so tight they were bleeding. Can your imagination fill in the blanks yet? You wanna know about the barn in Kentucky where I spent a week after I was sold to a farmer for a couple hundred bucks?"

I put the barrel of the 1911 between his eyes.

"You can be helpful to me or you can be a problem. I'll be nice if you help me, but I'm not afraid to kill you. What do the cops know about us?"

He smiled.

"I wasn't the captain of the football team. And I didn't go to prom. I had to work that weekend. You don't know a goddamned thing about me either," he said.

I lowered the gun and stubbed out the cigarette on his chest, then turned on the cold water and shut the door for a while.

The noise of the shower kept our conversations private, but we still whispered, even with the TV on. Ita had the channel switched to PBS. It was a documentary about a writer. He looked crazed. His eyes were wild. He spoke about the difficulty of writing and growing up poor. He had a thick Georgia accent. I was transfixed. Ita had to snap me out of it.

"What's his deal?"

"The cop?"

"No shit."

"He's a pile of bricks. I didn't get anything from him."

"I told you so."

"I know," I said, sipping my coke and whiskey through the straw. "Give him some more time and we'll see what happens."

"Or what doesn't happen."

"Right now, I just wanna watch this show."

"It's kind of boring," she said.

"I find it interesting."

She rolled her eyes. I kept watching the show about the author. He had a hard life. He had polio as a kid and fell into a hog-boil pit at the age of twelve. His flesh was permanently seared in places. His eyes were beady like a viper's staring out through a wrinkled, pulpy face like a mound of clay. He grew up in a shack with a single mother and a little brother as his sharecropper father died in the field from overwork. He talked about writing and life and disappointment.

I looked at Ita from the floor. She was sprawled out on the bed eating a cheeseburger.

"What do you think you would do if things had gone different for you?"

"I'd probably still be in Mexico," she said.

"No, I mean, what do you think you would do?"

She shrugged.

"I don't know. Work in a store? Work on an orchard."

"You don't think you'd do something else?"

"Like what?"

"Like an artist or a lawyer."

"You got to have the hook-up from birth to do things like that."

"Not this guy," I said, pointing to the TV.

"Aw. You wanna be a writer? That's so sad."

"I could write," I said. "I've read some books before."

"What books have you read?"

"I read..uh...I don't remember the name. It was a book about these two guys."

She laughed at me.

"I have read books, okay?"

"You missed the first part of the show," she said. "This weird guy said it's easier to be a brain surgeon than to be a writer."

I turned away and kept watching the show.

The author had a strange and interesting life. I stopped paying attention and started thinking about what it might take to write something down. I would need time, paper, maybe a computer. It seemed both within my reach and completely unattainable. Ita got up and went to the bathroom. She left the door open. The water pelted the cop's head, soaking through his white t-shirt, spraying onto the floor. She walked through the puddle and pulled her pants down and sat on the toilet. He didn't look at her. He just hung his head and shivered as the water came down. Ita stared at him while she pissed. When she was done she leaned over him and turned the water off. His chest was bruised black and purple. He seemed to breathe okay. Ita left the door open to keep an eye on him. She sprawled out across the bed behind me and massaged my shoulders from where I sat with my back against the bed.

"You're tense as hell."

"Yeah?"

"Your shoulders are as hard as rocks," she said, kneading my skin.

A commercial for humanitarian aid came on, showing children in makeshift hospital beds on the edge of a war zone. Their faces were gaunt like leather stretched over rocks. You could count the ribs above their inflated stomachs. They showed footage of soldiers pulling kids out of the rubble. I looked at the cop. He wasn't struggling to free himself. He just sat there.

Ita moved forward to karate-chop the muscles around my neck.

"Does that feel okay?"

"Yeah, I guess. It's numbing at least."

She stopped and I raised my head. She took the coke from my hands and had a sip.

"Hey, cop!" she said to him. "Hey, look at me."

He raised his head.

"You ever been shot before this?"

He shook his head.

"Us neither."

"You'll know what it feels like soon enough."

A moment of silence passed.

Ita turned back to the TV

"Oh, you ain't gonna try and get the last word like him there?"

"I don't have to try. I just did," she said, without looking away from the TV.

20

ta called me a cab to the laundromat and gave me a pair of shades and a roll of quarters. I didn't take the car in case something happened while I was out. I wanted her to have the car if she had to leave. When I got there, the machines didn't take quarters. You had to buy a prepaid card and swipe the reader for every cycle. I walked up to the desk in the corner. Where an old woman sat next to a list of prices. I walked up to the desk and set down my collapsible hamper.

"What's the $40 full service include?"

"We do the laundry and fold it for you," she said.

"Sounds good," I said, reaching for two twenties.

"It can take around an hour or more."

"I don't care," I said, handling her money.

I went behind the building to smoke a cigarette. There were broken washing machines piled along the back wall near the AC unit. I took a seat in a school desk someone had dumped in the weeds. The silos across the cow pasture were painted to look like soda cans with the trademark logos on the side: Cheerwine, Sun Drop, 7-Up.

I waited for a long time, letting my mind wander. When I went back inside where the clothes were waiting for me in the hamper, soft and clean and folded neatly and still warm from the dryer. I called the cab to come to pick me up and bought a small coffee from the vending machine. I waited on the curb with my clean clothes and sipped my coffee. The Blue Ribbon cab pulled up a little while later and I got inside with the hamper under my arm.

I got out and tipped the guy and walked up the winding concrete path to The Algodon. The shades were slipping off the bridge of my nose. I pushed them up as I noticed a girl leaning over one of the stucco arches. She had a nice face and she smiled at me. It looked like she was wearing somebody else's black leather jacket. Under that, she had on a white blouse, a gold necklace, and a pair of jeans. She kept smiling as I crossed her path.

"What is up?" she said, in an accent.

I nodded, acknowledging her.

"You got a cigarette?"

I paused and pulled the pack out of my jeans. I let her take one out of the pack herself.

"Thanks," she said.

I got a better look at her necklace. It said something in a foreign script.

"What's that?"

"My necklace?" she said, taking the cigarette. "It's my name."

"Where are you from?"

She lit a pink Bic and took the first inhale.

"I come from Tel Aviv."

"Israel," I said.

"Yes, you know it?"

I shook my head.

"Never been," I said, walking away. "I just used to stare at an atlas all the time."

She thanked me for the smoke as I turned the corner.

21

My initial plan with the Bible doesn't work. There are too many pages and they won't fold enough to fit inside. And I just finished hollowing the damn thing out. At least, I can still hide a gun in it. The lights are dead. The tap runs brown. I'm on my last bottle of liquor (a fifth of George Dickel) and my last pack of cigarettes (American Spirit Black). The room stinks of booze, body odor, and smoke. I can barely see the paper in front of me. My pen ran dry. I'm writing this with a pencil that I sharpen with the tactical blade. I ran out of coffee packets for the little machine on the dresser and risked heading out into the dark and flooded breezeway where the vending machines still hum and glow and blink and, in my soaked shoes and jacket, I bought a few cans of Mountain Dew. All my waking energy comes from soda, Adderall, and cigarettes. My sleep is a short coma from Valium boosted with liquor and room-temperature beer. I didn't recognize myself the last time I looked in the mirror. But I don't have to anymore.

We took turns, Ita and me (who else?), watching the Israeli girl. I thought she might have been a scout at first but she didn't know our room number or come looking for us after I gave her the cigarette. She was just a working girl. Different men, some who looked poor, some who were rich, came and went, parking their cars away from the office building and the main road. Ita floated the idea of killing her pimp for her, but the more we saw the more it seemed she was in business for herself, probably booking her johns online. We left her alone for the next night.

The cop shit himself, hoping we would untie him to clean him. We left him in the shower for a couple of hours but the stench got so bad that we ended up knocking him out by force-feeding him a bottle of Benadryl and cleaning him off in the shower. He woke up still drugged and slurring with fresh knots tying him to the chair.

I parted the blinds the same day and saw Ita sharing a beer and a smoke with the Israeli girl. I watched them for a few minutes and then laid down on the bed. She looked like she was having fun. I was happy for her. I dozed off without realizing it. When I woke up it was still light outside. Ita had invited the Israeli girl into our room for more beer. They were drinking and laughing and eating hummus with $2 gas-station tortillas on the edge of the bed where I lay. She was joking around and laughing and getting drunk and speaking Spanish (since the girl could speak it too) and we still had a goddamned police officer tied up without a gag in the bathroom. My eyes darted between the girls and the bathroom door. It was shut. I kept my cool, but I looked at Ita like she was crazy. When you're drinking beer, someone is eventually going to have to piss. The girl looked at me.

"Hey, remember this guy. We see us outside," she said in English.

Ita said something in Spanish and made the girl laugh. I didn't ask her what she said.

"Here," Ita said, switching to English. "Try this."

"I know what hummus is. I've eaten hummus before."

Ita laughed and ate it herself and said something else in Spanish. This time I asked the girl what she had said.

"She says you are a writer. You have high culture."

"She's making fun of me," I said.

"You don't write?"

I shook my head.

"No."

She looked at Ita.

"He looks like a writer. I don't know who is saying the truth."

"He wants to be a writer," Ita said.

"I know a writer once," she said.

"Yeah?"

"What was his name?"

"Pharat."

I stared at the bathroom door.

Ita wasn't looking at me. It was strange. Maybe she was too drunk. Maybe she didn't care anymore.

"Yeah," she said. "I know him in Tel Aviv. He lives in hotel. He stay in Israel so he don't go to jail."

"What did he write?"

"He shows me the books. I don't remember. I don't speak Turkish. He says he comes from Istanbul. He was sad. He pay me to sleep near to him for five days and then he went away. I never know what happen to him."

I tried to be diplomatic and get them out of the room, telling them I hadn't slept much the last few nights. Ita got up and walked toward the dresser. I did everything I could not to grab her shoulder as she drifted passed the bathroom door. My heart was racing. She poured me a coke and whiskey with ice from the bucket and reached over to hand it to me. The girl saw the fresh cuts along her arm

"What is happened to you? Who did this?"

Ita answered in Spanish.

The girl spoke better Spanish than English and responded. They talked for a while and I sipped the drink even though I didn't want it. The girl looked upset as they spoke. She rolled up Ita's sleeves and traced the callused lines and fresh razor slits in her skin, running her fingers up and down her arms. I set my drink down on the nightstand and stood up. I was further away from the bathroom now and staring out the window at the basketball court. I could see the girl's faint reflection in the dirty glass as she rummaged through her purse and took out some kind of salve or cream in a little tube. I looked at my transparent face then focused on the court across the street before adjusting again on the hovering ghost of the Israeli girl as she tended to Ita's wounds. I didn't know what she was saying as she applied the miracle cream to her cuts but I listened to her speak just the same. Ita wasn't smiling anymore. She stared down at the cuts on her forearms and whispered in Spanish. I closed the blinds and turned back to them.

"I need to sleep," I said, trying once more to get them out of the room before the son of a bitch got wise and started screaming for help.

The girl kissed the cuts on her arms and rolled her sleeves back down.

"Come on, let's go. He wants to be left alone."

Ita grabbed the hummus and chips and followed her to the door. They walked out onto the concrete veranda near the dusty sign of The Algodon. I took a deep breath and headed for the bathroom. The cop was passed out asleep in the empty tub. I didn't know when the chair had fallen over. I let him sleep.

Ita came back to the room alone just after the sun went down in that weird blueish stage (like the world is still adjusting to the shock of losing its light) before the total dark. She brushed her teeth, spit the blue foam on the cop as he slept, stripped down to her underwear, and crawled in bed beside me.

"You had fun with your girlfriend?"

"Does that make you jealous?"

"What if the cop started yelling for help?"

"What if? You shouldn't have kidnapped him in the first place. I don't give a shit one way or the other."

"I thought you told me that the fun was over?" I said.

She turned and shut off the lamp.

I got out of bed and went to the bathroom, closing the door behind me. The light was harsh on my eyes. I grabbed the back of the chair and slid the cop upright, waking him up. I put my hand on his shoulder and looked him in the eyes.

"You wanna tell me some things?"

He nodded.

"If you wanna accept the answers."

"When you drove up to ask for my license. Did you know who we were?"

"I still don't know who you are," he said. "But I figure you got the law after you if you're willing to shoot a cop?"

"I got worse than the law after me."

"Cartel?"

"Maybe."

"I didn't figure that."

"What do I have to do to get rid of you without killing you?"

He paused.

"Just cut me loose, man. I won't say shit about where we are or what you guys look like. I'll say you kept me in the trunk the whole time. Just cut me loose, man. You can drop me off in the woods. I'll give you a three-day head start. You can kamikaze to some jerkwater bordertown in Chihuahua for they even know. Don't kill me."

"You got kids?"

"No. No, I ain't got any kids. But I got a daddy on dialysis. I help pay his mortgage, man. I got a dog. I got a girl."

"Fair enough. I drop you out in the woods, you're not gonna develop a hero complex one the ride there? I'm gonna blindfold you and I'm gonna dump you and then...You'll be free."

He nodded.

"I won't do shit, man."

I slapped him on the shoulder.

"Hang tight," I said. "It's close to being over."

He didn't respond. He had this look on his face like I was going to shoot him right there, or maybe do it behind his back like the guy in that book I read a few years ago. I still can't remember the name. I shut the door on him and got back in bed. Ita was asleep.

I was in the middle of a nice dream. Ita was driving a van through an abandoned city where nature had returned. The alley off the sidewalk was dark below the tropical canopy that stretched between two tenement buildings. Roots and patches of tallgrass displaced the asphalt and concrete like slabs of glacial ice. The fallen bridges had become canyons and steel reinforcement beams hung like a vine. The van's engine backfired and I woke up in bed next to Ita. I heard the sound again and saw light pour through a fresh hole in the wall. Ita pushed me off the bed as she dove for the closet where she stashed the shotgun. I crawled to the corner of the room near the window and grabbed two pistols from the night stand and used a barrel of the 1911 to crack the blinds. There was a white pickup parked on the street and a man in a khaki vest and a flannel shirt used the side of the truck bed as a gunrest for a long bolt-action rifle. His face puckered as he squinted behind the black scope. There were two men in cargo pants and black masks crouching low beneath the steps across from our door.

Ita racked the shotgun and headed for the opposite window. The rifleman by the truck was only bait to get us close to the windows.

I told Ita to get back as the gunmen raised their Kalashnakovs. We crawled to the bathroom on our stomachs as the shooting started. It was louder than anything I had ever heard. Within the first few seconds, the rapid gunshots bled together into a single pulse. Plaster and glass dust rained down on our backs like streams of tear gas as the heavy rounds cut through the cheap building material. They stopped to reload and the ringing in my ears briefly replaced the drone of gunfire. The Two kicked in the front door and stormed the room. I didn't hear the lock burst from the wall or the debris crunch under their boots.

Ita lifted the shotgun and hit one in the chest, knocking him to the ground.

I flipped over on my back and started shooting. The surge of adrenaline felt like battery acid in my veins, corroding my arteries, and eating away at muscle tissue. The other one went down. His scalp burst apart in the hood of his fleece jacket. I still couldn't hear. My legs and arms shook. The cop was dead, shot more than ten times right through. There was so much blood it nearly covered the whole tub, stretching to the drain.

The man on the street tossed his rifle in the back of the truck and scrambled for the driver's seat. I picked up the heavy Kalashnikov and pressed the stock to my shoulder in the open doorway. I watched the muzzle flash without making a sound under the mild shade of the awning leaving behind bursts of smoke that carried into the morning light. The truck's tires deflated. The back window burst as the windshield fractured. He lost control and crashed into a shallow ditch.

Ita was not by my side. I turned and saw her feet sticking out from the bathroom. The dust had settled over her shins like talcum powder. Her toes twitched. I ran back to the bathroom. With every breath, the red puddle grew in the dip of her stomach until it soaked through the white fabric and seeped toward her hip bones. She was hit twice above the gut shot in her chest and once in the side of the face. It looked like the bullet had exited her throat. She was choking. I reached inside her throat to remove a broken molar and a shard of the splintered jawbone, but it didn't help. She gargled fresh blood and stared directly into my eyes. I don't know if she saw me or not. She kept looking at me after she stopped convulsing. I waved my hands in front of her face. I touched her forehead. I nudged her shoulders. She gave no response. Her gut shot stopped pulsating.

I stood up. I was covered in her blood. I took the other AK from the floor. The man Ita had hit with the buckshot was still clinging to life. I shot him with his weapon. The force of the bullets pushed his body an inch across the carpet kicking up ancient drywall dust and disintegrated plaster. I walked outside, shoeless, in my blood-soaked underwear and t-shirt. The truck's engine ran as it sat lopsided in the ditch, the rifleman lumped over the wheel. I reached into his pants pockets and took the cell phone. It was as big as a slate and the touch screen took up the entire front. His eyes rolled toward me and he mustered his last ounce of strength to reach inside his vest for the Glock in the leather shoulder holster. I backed up and fired the AK, nearly losing control. His body jerked back to the passenger's side and folded like a broken mannequin.

I grabbed out stuff and left. I didn't hear sirens this time but I still didn't linger. I didn't get dressed. I didn't wash off the blood. I took the keys and got in the car and drove. I drove through the backwoods where the rocks and tree limbs stuck out over the narrow, leafy road almost clipping my side mirrors. There were houses and odd little country sheds tucked high up in the reeds and crusty broom straw and hubcap-sized leaves growing out of lime-colored vines that strangled the crumbling rock faces. They looked out of place like they belonged in the tropics. Ita's blood dried and flaked within the creases in my knuckles, hands shaking on the steering wheel. When my hearing came back, I realized I had been screaming.

I screamed so hard I stopped in the middle of the road and threw up. I wiped my chin with the back of my wrist and got back in the car. By noon, I found a secluded creek with a few downed trees functioning as a bridge from the road to the ridge of massive boulders shining in the sun, the same gray color as elephant hide. I washed the blood off my body in the frigid water and, still shivering, pulled on my dry clothes. The heat still worked in the old Geo. I switched it on and smoked a cigarette as I fought off the cold. I was done screaming. My stomach felt like a bag of medical waste. As my ears adjusted and healed, I could hear myself as I wept over the shudder of the oil-starved engine. My eyes filled with tears. I could barely see the road. I stopped at an abandoned service station and watched a gathering of vultures picking at a dog carcass. The dog's tongue stuck out and its eyes were closed. The rib cage pierced the tangled gore of its lower abdomen.

The dead man's cell phone rang.

I hesitated before answering.

The ID on the touchscreen said "Motel Job."

I swiped with my thumb.

"Dale, how are we?"

The voice was familiar.

"Was that his name?" I said. "Dale? Farmer type? How much did you pay him?"

"Who is this?"

"You don't remember my voice? I remember yours."

He paused.

"I can hear a change in you, Basil. How's this life you've chosen treating you?"

I ignored the question.

"The guys you keep sending appear to be failing," I said.

"You sound tired. Hoarse, like you've been running. You have been running, haven't you? Like an animal. You know how some animals wheeze when they're panicked, when they're backed into a corner? Basil, I came down here to clean some things up, to get the books balanced, but I've underestimated the situation. I'm not above admitting that. You're a consistent problem. Congratulations. But If you think I've lost control-"

I cut him off.

"Control? You want to talk about control. Cops are headed to the place where your contract rednecks are lying dead next to the body of the missing police officer from TV. And get this, we might have tied him up, but your boys were the ones that killed him. They can trace bullets, right? Once they clear the rubble and find one of their own murdered...There's no putting the lid back on that one. You wanna talk about control? You never had it, you Russian-American, pinko fuck! Because I never had anything to lose."

"Everyone has something to lose," he said, calmly.

"Not me. Not anymore."

"You didn't let me finish," he said. "It's an old adage my grandpa taught me back in Detroit. He said he learned it in a gulag. It was a prison in Siberia they sent him to after he fought the Nazis in World War II. His captain taught it to him. He said, "Everyone has something to lose. And if they don't, then you start with their feet.""

22

I drove up that dark, familiar highway to the mountains where a massive cloud of steam from the nuclear facility wafted through either side of the winding asphalt strip. The trees had shed their leaves. I stopped off at a Waffle House for anything that might settle my stomach. I looked crazy scanning the diner with haunted eyes from my corner booth. The truckers and lumber yard workers and old lays fresh out of church did what they could to ignore me. A middle-aged man, simple in the head, wandered away from his elderly caretaker or mother or whatever she was to him and started setting wrapped peppermints from his starched church pants pockets on the edge of everyone's table. The old woman he sat with didn't go after him. She just drank her coffee, a look of indifference or perhaps defeat on her withered face. He gave me a cheeky, genuine smile as he dropped off the candy and, for one second, I wasn't the focus of the diner staff and local patrons. I paid for my Texas melt and ice water and left. I could hold the last bit of our cash in one hand without stretching my fingers. I needed to ditch the car but I didn't know where to start. I should have asked Ita more about the chop shops when I had the chance. Somewhere along the drive, I decided I'd gotten enough revenge and since the inevitable finally took Ita. I didn't see the harm in giving myself the easy way out. Obviously, I was going to use a gun, but I didn't want to just do it anywhere. I drove out to our old rendez-vous point on the parkway. As I pulled into the lot, I saw the black 1967 Imperial with the popped hood still sitting there with cobwebs around the tires, leaves in the engine. I couldn't remember if she threw away the keys or not. I parked in the adjacent space and stared at it for a while. I made a wager with myself. If I still had the keys to the Imperial in Ita's stuff, I would switch cars and the killing, the real killing. If I didn't, I could rest. I rummaged through our things, searching for an extra pair of keys. I came up empty. I was relieved anyway. I walked out to the place where tourists took pictures against the view. They say if you give yourself an out, you don't really want to go through with it. I fully intended to die that day, but I'm not one to disrespect a miracle either. I gave myself a chance because Ita's car, against all logic, was still there. I took out the revolver I liked from the back of my jeans. I checked the cylinder to make sure it was loaded. The sun was setting. The sky was pink. As a shadow, I pressed the short barrel to my temple and pulled the trigger.

The gun jammed, producing an impotent, metallic click.

I leaned over the railing and threw up my Texas melt. I never kept up the guns the way Ita did and as a result, my favorite pistol jammed. I tossed it off the cliff. I walked back to the parking lot, defeated, resurrected. I stared at the black Imperial again. I got closer and reached for the door handle. It popped open. She had left the goddamned thing unlocked. I sat down behind the steering wheel. I looked at the dash and fiddled with the sun visor overhead.

A set of keys dropped into my lap.

You don't disrespect a miracle.

I got my things and loaded the trunk and put a small Glock and the 1911 in the glove box. I adjusted the rearview mirror and saw my own bloodshot eyes. I talked to myself and gave myself a smile. The spirit of Tsala was with me. I had a killer's blood running through my veins.

23

A nice kid with a Browning insignia on his baseball cap and bright orange freckles all over his face at the gun shop sold me a Kevlar Systems bullet-proof vest and a SecPro IIIA Ballistics mask and since I wasn't buying ammunition (I had plenty) or a gun he didn't ask for an I.D. I drove another forty minutes south into Beaufort where the air had that familiar salty odor and parked in the strip club parking lot. It would end where it began. I strapped on the vest and made sure the three guns I was carrying were loaded. I had never used the shotgun before and I worried I wouldn't be able to control it. I pulled on the black mask. It was featureless and only protected the front of my head excluding the eye holes. I took a few deep breaths and walked toward the entrance. They didn't keep the doorman right at the entrance like most places. You had to enter and walk down a dark hallway where the pounding music got louder and louder. But there wasn't any music today. It was too early. I was surprised the door was unlocked. I moved down the hallway as the bright light of the midday sun shining through the glass entrance quickly faded, sticking close to the black carpeted wall, silent, letting my eyes adjust to the increasing darkness. Gaudy pink neon and hot white, moon-surface stage lights brightened the frigid AC-controlled chasm of the dancefloor and black vinyl booths. There was a new bouncer I didn't recognize lounging behind the DJ table before his shift. He sipped from a gold-rimmed glass of Rize çayi. I had the shotgun strap around my shoulder. I didn't want to start with something so loud with that much firepower. I pulled out an ugly little Chinese copy of a Glock, a throwaway, gestured toward the sound system, and then aimed the barrel squarely between his eyes. He dropped the Turkish tea and, shaking, reached his hand over to the sound system. The song blasted through the speakers. I stood in front of him listening to chattering hi-hats and snare hits. The song began to crescendo. He moved to the right the moment the base dropped, muting the gunshot and tearing his face apart. His nose and upper lip had been removed by the force of the bullet, exposing his bone and gums and teeth. He was still breathing. I shot him again. The pop of the gun was audible over the music. The left side of his face flattened against the ground. The blood poured out so fast his entire upper body was taken up by the shallow pool within seconds. I headed for the back door where the counting room was closed off from the rest of the club. I shot the lock off the door and kicked my way through. There was already an aged Albanian man in a sweatsuit at the ready with a .357 Magnum. He took one shot that sailed past my face and I gave him three to the chest in return. I swung out through the next threshold and killed a boy holding a shiny nickel-plated automatic sideways. I emptied the rest of the Glock. He fell backward on the portable Coleman folding table covered in paperwork and wrinkled bundles of dull green cash. His arm hung to the side as the pistol dropped to the floor. He stared up at the fluorescent lights, motionless. I pulled out the 1911 and flicked the safety and racked the slide as I crossed through the dressing rooms. Two girls, still in plain clothes hid, below the makeup tables with their hands over their heads. I opened the last door as the light flooded into the dressing room. A younger-looking man with dress pants and a rug-pattern, silk shirt was doing his best to climb over the chainlink fence with a Tech-9 in one hand. He turned and aimlessly sprayed as he fell from the fence onto the concrete. The rapid-fire ricocheted off the brick and rusted steel of the dumpster. I shot him six times as he lay there against the weeds and chainlink. I walked back through the club, pocketing some of the money for the road, and left through the entrance. There was no one left. I flipped the ballistic mark over my head as I approached the car. I hadn't even used the shotgun. I popped the trunk open and started throwing everything inside. I unfastened the first strap on the vest when a bullet flattened against the kevlar in the center of my spine. The momentum knocked me forward. I reached for the stock of the shotgun and turned to see the bastard who shot me. It was a kid, a fresh age-out made foot soldier just like me. I said, "Do you want to be the one who tells them what went down? Or one of the bodies they hide in the concrete?" He made his decision and so did I.

24

did the only thing I knew how to do. I drove. I drove back North for hours and stopped in a little mountain town in Kentucky to sleep at a rest stop because I had lost my fake I.D. No cop stopped me. No caretaker, no trucker tapped on my window to bother me, to stir me awake. I went to a strip mall off the interstate and paid cash at a Men's Warehouse for a suit and substantial coat for the frigid cold. The salesgirl was nervous when she talked to me and the Korean woman manning the fitting station appeared disgusted by how I smelled. I could see her face in the mirror. They probably thought I was homeless, buying a suit for some church gathering or wedding on charity from my estranged family.

I left Kentucky and crossed the Ohio for the fourth time in my life. I drove into Brazil that late afternoon. It didn't look anything like I remembered it but I was still able to find my old street. The home was smaller to me now with a crumbling brick doorstep like a punched-in smile. Trash bags were piled near the mailbox. The name read "Laneko," my mother's maiden name. There was a chained-up barking dog near the trailer in the adjacent lot. I followed the familiar trees to my uncle's place. There were plywood boards on the window and front door. The light was already starting to fade and the street lights came on the minute I killed the engine. I got out and looked at the place, at the porch, the evergreen in the front yard, the dilapidated roof.

An old black woman was sweeping her porch next door. She didn't engage until I asked her about Mr. Shaver. She looked away from the concrete and sized me up. I didn't look like family, I didn't even look black, but she asked if I was family anyway. Maybe she remembered the little bronze kid I used to be. I nodded and told her I was family. She paused and told me Mr. Shaver left after the bank foreclosed on his house in '08.

I asked her if she knew where he lived now.

She shook her head and shrugged.

I thanked her anyway and returned to my childhood home. Whoever lived there hadn't bothered to scrape the name off the mailbox. I wanted to put a cigarette in my mouth and just stand in the dying light watching the house but I found myself following another even more physical compulsion and walked up to the doorstep and rang the yellow-plastic doorbell. What was I going to say? I just wanted to see another face, to hear another person's voice even if they told me to fuck off. I wasn't going to find my uncle. I wanted to see someone. I waited at the door. A raspy woman's voice yelled out from the opposite end, shuffling, feet scratching against an abrasive carpet. The deadbolt retracted and the chain swung off the slide. The door opened. A familiar woman in her mid-forties stood on the threshold with a PPG industries logo on her work uniform, an unlit cigarette sat in the notch of her ear saved for later. She sniffled and paused and didn't say anything else.

I stared into her eyes.

She attempted to speak but I shook my head and set my finger to her lips.

A man's voice bellowed from the front room.

"Who is it?"

She finally said something.

"Are you…"

I nodded.

"It's me," I said.

I pushed past her and walked inside. She was still with the same guy who left me at the Circle Center in Indianapolis. He was sitting on the couch in front of the TV with a dog on his lap and a beer in his hand. The mutt shepherd mix growled at me.

"You all came back to Brazil," I said.

"We hired a private detective!" she said, still shaking in the doorway. "We hired a detective."

I paced in the room.

The dog's eyes followed me. So did his.

I scratched my nose and turned off the flatscreen.

"You sent a detective? A private detective? Hmm. I guess that counts for something," I said. "You could have come looking for me. I walked around downtown Indy for a week. You had a week to get me back. You didn't come looking. I guess I didn't want to be found anyway. What did your private detective turn up? Anything?"

Her boyfriend didn't say. He watched me, stunned, the dog in his lap, a beer in his hand.

"Yeah, I didn't think so," I said. "You guys know where my uncle is? Where did he go after his house was foreclosed on?"

Silence.

"I came here to see him," I said. "Not you. I just want to see my uncle."

I could feel myself start to shake.

My mom's boyfriend, or perhaps husband by now, gave me a disgusted look and finally moved, setting his beer down on the table.

"We don't know where he is," he said.

"You don't know?"

"We don't know," he said, pausing for a moment. "He didn't come to look for you either."

I drew the pistol in my coat pocket and shot him and the dog. His body went limp. The dog spasmed and whimpered as it died. My mother screamed and placed her hands over her ears for whatever reason, probably none. I shot her just above the eyes and she fell back into the open doorway. I stepped over her body as I left for the car.

25

On the TV, the eyewitnesses described me as a thin man with a dark vehicle that looked like a hearse and a long black coat. Just like that, I became The Man in Black, or The Angel of Death depending on which channel you watched. People were afraid they'd look out their windows and see a classic black sedan pulling into their driveway. An unemployed plumber in Terre Haute shot his neighbor, a 25-year-old immigrant from Mexico, to death for driving across the street in a newly restored jet-black Pontiac Bonneville.

For days, I hid in the abandoned office kiosk behind the tarnished screen of a long gone drive-in movie lot. I stashed the Imperial under a weather tarp in the tall reeds. My only connection to the outside was the smartphone and I was careful not to run out the battery or the data. I was careful not to build a fire during the day and to at least hide the glow of the flames in the burn barrel half in and half out of the kiosk. At night, I pretended to watch movies on the back of the giant screen, movies about Ita driving down the highway in a convertible letting her hair dance in the wind. Freezing rain fell most nights.

I slept huddled against the barrel in my coat and fine suit like a horror villain when the cameras aren't rolling, haunting the drive-in grounds from some cliched legend. I watched squirrels and stray cats in the morning frost and imposed my narrative onto movements, making up feuds between them to occupy my mind. I did that and I thought back to the last book I had read. I still couldn't remember the title; a thin, short book, easy to read, about two men on the west coast who find work in an orchard. It was so good I remember thinking it was the only book. But I'm not stupid. You can tell from my words and my remembering all of this that I'm not stupid. I always did good in school for the short time I went and I became a closet autodidact in my whore days. I stole books from bedside tables and store shelves when I could. I thought about the dog I shot at my mother's house and the old scrappy dog they killed in the middle of the last book I had read all those years ago and then I thought about how the book ended.

I hid out until my cache of food ran dry. I had nothing else to fight the cold with except for my instantly recognizable coat, so I took it with me despite the danger, but I left the Imperial behind as I walked to a highway rest stop to steal a car. Slowly, I left the drive-in. I left my miracle car. I left the still-rolling image of Ita in her full movie star gown in that black and white and steely silver screen reel of gossamer footage and I had a bag of loose clothes and a booze bottle and ammunition and one thick shotgun stretching its polyester and nylon ends like a homeless mercenary on a cold-June death march through southern Africa.

I found a rest stop just as the light morning rain started to freeze. I wasn't used to this cold. I could see my breath. I covered my mouth with my coat lapel as I hid behind a tree to search for a victim to carjack. I watched families stop in minivans and buy soda from the vending machines and use the bathrooms. Elderly couples stopped and let their small dogs shit in the field past the frozen picnic tables. I felt like crying. I held back the tears. Truckers and hard-looking men stopped as well. I needed someone who didn't look like they might have had a gun or a pocket constitution on them at all times. I waited in the cold like a monster.

26

The Man in Black, or The Angel of Death, The Indiana Twilight Stalker, The Door-to-Door Killer, The Brazil Killer, The Imperial Killer, The Real-Life Slender Man, The Hearse Driver, The Unknown Suspect took his victim on that wet frosty day on the Indiana interstate.

His name was Dalton Stahl. He was a twenty-two-year-old college student from DePauw University up in Greencastle. He was born in Budapest, Hungary, and grew up in Louisville, Kentucky. He wrote poetry in his spare time and played the saxophone. He was Jewish, non-practicing, and a self-identified atheist. He liked to drink beer and smoke marijuana as much as possible. He enjoyed hiking and listening to classic jazz and hip-hop. He was gay and still a virgin at twenty-two. He was tall for his age and skinny. He had a slight lisp when he spoke. He drove his mother's gray, 2018 Ford EchoSport. I sat in the back of the car and drank my liquor with one hand and, with the other, pressed the pistol against the back of the driver's seat with my finger flat on the trigger guard. He cried behind the wheel even though I wasn't going to kill him. I didn't *want* to kill him. I didn't want to kill someone who had done nothing. I didn't want to scare him either. I just wanted to get drunk and get a ride out of the state.

The headline would say 'The Ride from Hell' once he talked to the police and the news channels. He drove me down through Kentucky and back into Tennessee. It was a road I had traveled all my life. I knew it like the back of my hand. I would never escape it. The kid never really calmed down but he did get quiet and he eventually struck me as somewhat brave. He never stopped believing that I was going to kill him. I saw it in his face. I got pretty drunk and I asked him all kinds of questions about his life. I told him about my life and I told him about my ancestor Tsala Freeman, the reason I came back to Indiana in the first place. I told him he could play music if it would make it easier. I didn't like his music but I allowed it. We made it through the mountains with some serious weather behind us, a snowstorm for the century. I saw the Welcome to North Carolina sign through the falling snow and close to midnight the highway traffic stalled. I lit a cigarette in the back of his mom's car and looked at him in the rearview mirror. We were ten feet away from a highway exit to a small town on the edge of the Biltmore Estate, a giant mansion where people took pictures of themselves and their families. I could almost see the Huddle House diner through the gathering blizzard.

"Well, Dalton. I think this is where I make my stop."

"You're gonna walk through this?"

I left him a thousand dollars and the rest of the whiskey. I grabbed my bag and walked out into the snow, stepping over the steel highway guard and into the woodland separating the interstate from the town toward the warmth of the 24-hour diner.

27

hid the bag under the dumpster behind the diner before
heading around to the front and walked inside.

"Are you open?"

"We're closing in an hour?" the girl passing me said.

"An hour? If you can't drive now you won't make it an
hour from now. What's the difference?"

I talked too much when I was drunk. I'm sure they could
smell the potent whiskey on my breath.

"We don't make the decisions," a grill cook said. "An hour
from now will give us enough of a shot to go home before it
melts to slush and freezes over. Bossman orders."

A man with a cowboy hat added his worthless two cents.

"It's all gonna be ice in the morning. Cars will skid off the
roads. Power lines will go down."

"Can I get a cup of coffee for the road?"

"You can get whatever you want for the road," the girl
said, nodding toward the empty booth. She was tiny with a
short face and a long, boney neck, straight reddish brown hair,

and an unusually small waist. She had wrapped the ties around her hips more than once just to get her apron to fit.

I sat down and pulled out the smartphone. I had made it out of Indiana clean. The girl came back with my coffee and the glass of water I hadn't asked for. I warmed up and watched the snow outside. I didn't eat anything. For some reason, I wasn't hungry. Over the hour, the other patrons left, driving away into the gathering snow. I picked myself up and went back around to the dumpster. I got down on my knees in the wet snow and pulled the bag out.

"What the fuck are you doing?"

The girl from inside was standing there in the cold, smoking a cigarette. She was small and hard to see in the dark. She could have been a parking meter.

"I'm getting my stuff," I said. "I didn't want to bring it inside?"

"Why?"

"Cause it looks suspicious."

"Okay," she said, weirded out.

"It's my clothes and stuff."

"Okay," she said and walked away after flicking the cigarette. She looked a little shook.

I threw the bag over my shoulder and went down the sidewalk. The snow crunched under my feet. I felt the cold in my bones. I started to feel the paranoia set in. Had the girl recognized me from the TV? Not me, but the description, The Man in Black. I trekked through the snow, the scattered flakes catching me in the eye. I passed beneath the frozen street lights and imagined a police cruiser rolling up behind me, the snow turning red and flashing blue. But it never came. I was alone. I was always alone. I started to wonder if I could freeze to death.

28

've had to write some of this with my left hand. My other hand started cramping up and sometimes, when I hold the disappearing pencil, I feel a sharp pain in my wrist and thumb. The skin right below my thumb is numb. I thought it was nerve damage from alcohol abuse, but I think it's just from writing non-stop. I'm writing to you in a way that hurts and a way that makes everything seem real again. I want to get the details in because I want this to be as real as it can be and I want it to be honest. Just lay it out straight like it is. Except, I've figured out that it's not always straight, not always straight-forward. I can say what I did and how it happened and what I thought and what things looked like and smelled like and felt like, but I can't lay them out completely right because if something was going to be laid out completely right, the way it happened, it wouldn't have me talking about how it felt after the fact.

I can't tell you anything other than what I did.

So maybe this is art or something.

Or maybe it's just hundreds of pages of bullshit.

I wish now that I had some kind of a recorder to talk into. It would save my hand from hurting. Maybe if I had a recorder, I'd be finished by now. It hadn't hit until now, even when I did it, even when I wrote it down, not when I was in my new clothes in the snow in North Carolina, but as I'm writing this down on the yellow paper right now, it hadn't sunk in all the way that I killed my mother. I murdered my mom. I hadn't seen her in years and I showed up on her doorstep and killed her.

I've seen a lot.

I watched Ita die. I saw the cop die. And the same bullets somehow didn't hit me. Then I failed to kill myself. I can't even go on my terms. Is there anything left? Do I find religion, or do I start one?

What else can I tell you about the snow in North Carolina? It would have been something if that Waffle House girl found me in the snow and gave me a ride that night, maybe trusted me enough to let me crash on her couch. She'd turn out to understand my situation and help me, realizing what I was up against. But that didn't happen. I was alone all night in the cold until I found a warm exhaust grate beside a downtown government building and slept there, homeless, for the whole night. I wish I hadn't left the kid's car. In the morning, I got up and warmed myself at a truckstop burger king and ate and drank even more coffee, this time with the bag of guns under the plastic chair. I suppose I didn't care anymore. I could have been arrested right there in the shop. A cop could have walked inside and matched the description. I remember almost asking to hitch a ride with one of the long-haul guys but decided it was too risky to draw attention to myself like that. I had to get rid of the outfit.

I found a store not too far down the street and I bought myself a different wardrobe and slightly more practical jacket, something with layers and pockets. I got myself a hat too and better pants and shoes. I looked more like a hiker now, a drifter. I *was* a drifter.

I tried to get a greyhound bus ticket and the lady asked me for a photo I.D. I acted like I needed to get it out of my bag and stepped out of line and walked away. I walked to the South Carolina border and slept in a library until they kicked me out. My beard was growing nearly full and I started to look worn down by the cold and the street. I couldn't sleep at a homeless shelter with my arsenal in tow.

I found the local train depot and camped out for a day watching everything, studying the patterns. I had no idea what I was doing. I slept overnight beneath a highway overpass, bundled in everything I had. It was still cold even in South Carolina. The next day I caught a freighter that was heading down, getting me that much closer to the coast again. The shipping containers were red and said "Hamburg Süd" on the side. My ass picked up a brown diamond pattern from sitting on the rusted grating on my end of the train car and the last flecks of yellow paint came off with my hand on the railing. On the train, you could see all the land rushing past you instead of the next license plate like on the highway. On the road, you caught flashes of the margins of things: dead deer, flattened coyotes, broken down cars, garbage tossed at the wood's edge. The train showed you everything you didn't see, all the parts of life you wished you saw more of. I saw birds following the horizon. I waved to kids in trailer parks as they raced the boxcars with switches in their hands like primitive spears. The world behind me didn't disintegrate into a vacuum. It grew slowly, expanding into itself. It was great, but it wasn't worth the last few cold nights.

The train halted just outside Florence once and then made a stop close to Myrtle Beach. I left the railyard and scaled the vine-covered chain link. There was a tent city at the bottom of the slope, close to a small pond. Fires were pushing smoke up to the leafless treeline. The squatters had thrown up a few ropes between the pines where their clothes hung, drying hard in the wind. I walked almost a full two hours before I hit the beach and sat down to rest my legs on the boardwalk. The tourist season was over but the long strand was still crowded with people in windbreakers flying kites, walking their dogs, loitering. I blended in with the crowd like any other coastal vagrant. A guy in a black hoodie approached me. I felt my chest tighten. I reached into my coat pocket and took hold of the pistol grip. He made eye contact and showed me an old Mp3 player.

"Hey, man. You wanna buy this?"

I told him to fuck off and he drifted down the boardwalk. I walked to the edge of the surf and stared at the greenish-brown ocean. Despite the wind, pelicans were still diving out of the sky for fish; seagulls were still screaming. I wandered along the beach until I lost sight of the boardwalk. The strip didn't end and I took a right, walking back through the trees and dunes when I found an uneven sidewalk. The sandy concrete led me past a few shacks and trailers covered in pine needles. I didn't see bottle trees and brick dust on the door fronts here, I wasn't far enough south. I found a road and followed it to a palm-lined boulevard in a part of town where no building reached higher than a single floor and fresh seafood was advertised in hand-painted letters across their exposed cinder blocks. I tried to stay off the main roads, crossing alleys and gravelly back lots. Dogs barked in caged-off yards. There weren't many people out and the ones that saw me paid me no mind. I came to an intersection with a couple of row houses and a liquor store. I went in to buy myself a bottle of whiskey and the clerk denied me since I didn't have an I.D. There were a couple of girls working the corner. I flashed the nearest one a hundred and she followed me between a couple of oaks in a side lot. She looked cold with her tank top and exposed midriff inside the open white jacket and thin, bleached-white jeans Her weave was long and straight with a few strands of neon pink along the cropped bangs. I put the money in her hand and told her she could keep the rest if she went inside and bought me a couple of tallboys and a bottle of whiskey. She held the Benjamin up against the gray sky as if that would show her something and asked if the bill was real.

"Of course, it's real."

"Can I get myself something?"

"Sure."

She came back with a black plastic bag dangling from her right hand and a brown paper sack over the wine-bottle shape in her left. I thanked her and took out the pint of whiskey. We clinked the glass of our bottles together.

"Here's to sleeping rough," I said.

"I don't sleep rough."

"Not you. Me," I said.

She took a swig from the blue mouth of the bottle and screwed the cap back on.

"I gotta go now," she said.

I watched her leave before I put the alcohol in my bag. I didn't want her to see the guns and the money.

29

My bum days came to an end one morning on the beach. I was staying in dunes where raccoons crawled around me every night, fighting for loose trash. I slept under a tarp to protect myself and to keep my clothes and camping store sleeping bag as immaculate as I could in the shifting sands. Two weeks on, I woke up, still drunk, and heard the smartphone buzzing. Along with the outdoor gear, I bought a drugstore cord so I could charge the phone when I found a free outlet. Since then, I got into the habit of leaving it on all night. I lifted the screen to see who was calling a dead man. The I.D. said "Motel Job" again.

"My old friend, have you been replaced yet?"

"I was sitting here hoping you wouldn't answer."

"What? Did you think I had gone to prison?"

"I'd know if you were in prison. And you would already be dead."

"I know," I said.

"If you think we'll stop hunting you just because you brought the police to our door, you're wrong."

"I know that too."

"Did your bitch know it?"

"If you thought we had any kind of goal of a getaway plan with this, then you're the one who's wrong. It has always been suicide. That's all it ever was."

"How come you're still alive?"

"It isn't in my hands," I said.

"Do you believe in God?"

I rubbed my face and sniffled.

"You know, Itendahui used to ask me that all the time. I always said no. But I'm thinking about becoming a believer just so I know there's a hell for you to go to."

He laughed.

"You come up with that all by yourself?"

"I did," I said.

"Enjoy the beach."

The call disconnected.

I dropped the phone and checked my back. I stood up and looked over the dunes before packing up my makeshift camp. I tore the phone apart and stuck it in the white sand.

The city looked empty that morning. The street lights were still on.

I didn't see the van until I turned the corner at the empty market grounds. It was the same black van from the motel on the outer banks. The driver was heading to the public beach, following the signal when they caught me crossing the road. He cut the wheels and the van nearly careened onto its side. I ran like hell. I had my weapons on me but needed to buy myself some time, time to set up everything. The adrenaline killed the effects of my morning drunk and the lingering sickness gave me a kind of throbbing, painful focus. I know this was it and, sadly, I was relieved that I was going to die now. This time, I was the only target they'd be shooting at. But I was still going to make it painful for them.

I passed through the brick arch into a cemetery and followed the mulched path to the mausoleum. The wrought-iron gates were chained shut. When they came for me, I could see each one of them as they passed through the same archway. I threw my bag against the old limestone and took out the Tech-9 first. I checked my only magazine and set it aside and then propped the shotgun against the wall. I stuffed the 1911 into the crotch of my pants and took out the Glock with its extra magazines and tucked them into my coat pockets. The last thing I did was put on the ballistics mask. I didn't bother with the vest. I was ready to go.

I thought the cemetery was empty. I scanned the hill past the mausoleum. And old man was sitting on the park bench in a tweed jacket and a straw hat, talking to himself in a foreign language as he twirled the handle of a bamboo cane. I waved him down and he looked up and saw my eerie featureless mask and weapons. I motioned for him to leave. He stood up and limped away as fast as he could.

The van parked in front of the gate and the sliding door opened just enough for the barrel of a silencer to emerge out of the open space. I watched them for a few moments without making the first move. I had some kind of high ground and cover. I picked up the Tech-9. It was a strange feel compared to the other pistols. The front was heavy. I wrapped my free hand around the magazine like a grip.

Two men exited the van with thick black pistols fitted with silencers. They took cover behind the brick pillars. I started shooting. The gun kicked like hell. I shot away deep red clods of the brick and put some aluminum-colored holes in the side of the van. I was only marking my territory and wasting rounds at this point. The driver leaped out of the front seat and came to the edge of the gate with a compact AK-47 copy and let his entire magazine go against the mausoleum wall to drive me back. The men with pistols ran forward, climbing the small hill. I sprayed eight shots with one hand before the Tech-9 jammed. I picked up the shotgun and hit the driver through the gate. The buckshot rang against the iron. I adjusted the mask to see better. The driver had caught a few pellets in his left leg and hand. He limped behind the van. The other two were hiding behind stone obelisks. I pumped another round into the chamber and watched them. They moved one at a time, creating cover for themselves as they attempted to distract me. The bursts from the shotgun kept kicking up dirt and stone dust. We had reached an impasse.

I heard sirens in the distance: Myrtle Beach PD.

The driver crawled back to the front of the van and pulled the door open. I fired a few more rounds of buckshot and failed to hit anything. I was out of shells. I caught a muzzle flash from the side of the obelisk and took a direct shot to the center of my cheek. The outer shell split from the impact of the bullet as the woven kevlar frayed. It felt like taking a full swing from a sledgehammer with nothing but the brim of a baseball cap to cushion it. The eyehole had warped shut. I ripped off the mask so I could see.

The driver started honking as the engine turned.

The police sirens were headed down the street.

They retreated, firing off a few last rounds for cover.

I grabbed my bag and took off into the trees leaving the busted mask, empty shotgun, and jammed Tech-9. I jumped the shorter portion of the perimeter wall and slowed my walk as I crossed the storm drain up to the road. I hid behind a church playground as I took the nickel-plated 1911 out of my pants and stashed it along with the Glock and loose magazines. I lit a cigarette as I strolled through the neighborhood. It took a while for the sirens to fade as I put as much distance between me and the cemetery as I could without looking like I was fleeing. I finished the cigarette and lit a fresh one with the burning filter. That's when I realized my hand was covered in blood. I looked down and saw the blood trickling from my sleeve, leaving a jagged line of deep red splotches on the concrete behind me.

♦

30

felt the heat first and then, as nausea set in from blood loss, once the shock wore off, I felt the circumference of the wound. I had taken a bullet just above the crook of my elbow close enough to the outside of my shoulder that I thought they might have only grazed me, but the pain suggested otherwise. I didn't know what getting shot was supposed to feel like. Was I supposed to feel the mashed lump in my tissue? I dragged myself along a reedy ditch beside a massive steel drainage tunnel and collapsed in a familiar lot. It was the same liquor store. My vision was starting to go. Everything had a pink and yellow aura. I took out a dirty T-shirt and tried to build some kind of tourniquet.

I heard a voice from behind the oak tree.

"Mr. Hundred-Dollar bill."

It was the working girl in all white again. She stepped into my impared view as she sipped from a bottle of Coke. She came closer and got a better look at the shape I was in.

"Oh, shit."

"I got shot," I said.

"Yeah, I can see."

I took my clean hand and pulled out a wad of cash. It was almost everything I had.

"I need to get off the street. I got people after me."

"You need an ambulance is what you need."

"No ambulance," I said, shoving the money in her face. "If I go to the ER, they'll find me. It's not the police," I said, lying to her.

"If I don't call 911, you'll die anyway."

"I don't care about dying. I just don't want them to win," I said, except I did care about dying. At that moment, I realized I didn't want to die because I still wanted to kill the man on the other end of those phone calls.

I kept my good hand extended, offering her the money.

"Please," I said.

She hesitated.

"I haven't hurt anyone who was innocent," I said, lying again.

She pocketed the cash.

"Let's try not to bloody up my jacket if we can," she said. "I'm gonna stick my neck out just this once."

"Help me rip this T-shirt. I'm too weak."

I handed her the T-shirt. She tore down the middle and tied off the wound as well as she could. I hurt worse than the gunshot. Every nerve was on fire. She put the Coke bottle up to my lips and told me to chug as much as I could.

"Why?"

"You need something to offset the dizziness. I've seen it before and I need you to walk. I can't carry you."

I drank the Coke and tried to pull myself together.

"I'm going to help you up now," she said.

My fingertips were numb.

"Get my bag," I said.

She hoisted me as I slid against the back wall. My knees locked. I took a step forward.

"Can you do it?"

"I can do it."

She led me through a few backyards covered in pine needles and held me back as a few cars passed by on a one-way street. I staggered forward through the ivy and brush and we passed through the screen door to her small duplex home. I collapsed on her concrete patio.

When I came to, there was an angry, shirtless man with latex clothes staring at me.

"The first 30 minutes are critical and I did everything I can do, but you might still die if you have shrapnel from the bullet inside you, or you get an infection like blood poisoning," he said. "And I'd appreciate it if you didn't die on my cousin's couch."

I passed out again.

I think I dreamed then and in my dream, the girl had made me a necklace out of the crushed bullet from my arm.

I woke up on an old couch in an otherwise empty room. The side of the cushion and the dishwater-colored rug were stained with my blood. I was wearing my T-shirt (also caked in blood) with a crude gauze wrap on my lower shoulder. The girl walked over, smoking an E-cig.

"Do you have HIV?"

"I don't think so but I don't know for sure."

"HEP-C?"

"I don't know."

"You're lucky I brought my cousin here. And you're lucky I made him leave too. He's army. He stitched you up. Said there wasn't no bullet to find. Exit wound. Your odds were alright before you decided to come here of course. We did what we could to clean the wound the…"

I cut her off.

"You're cousin. He a snitch?"

"He's family."

"The fuck does that mean?"

"He won't snitch."

She paused and exhaled the saccharine vapor.

"I need you gone soon. Otherwise, I'll need more money, okay?"

"You connected?"

"To what?"

"I need a fake I.D. I'll pay you extra."

31

spent the next four days either sleeping, or staring at the ceiling while she was in her bedroom getting fucked by johns. She wasn't kind, but she didn't need to be. Opening up her home and playing battlefield hospital for a few grand was kind enough. It was more than I could have hoped for. She had another cousin who could forge a convincing driver's license. He was young, maybe only 16, and I traded him the 1911 pistol for his services. My new name was Mathew Greene and I was from Aiken, South Carolina.

After four days, I could sit up and walk around the room which meant it was time to leave. I thanked her before I left and she gave back my jacket with a new Carolina Panthers iron-on patch hiding the bullet hole. It was as if she had done this all before. I apologized for the bloodstains on the carpet and couch and offered her more money. She refused and I left.

My arm was raw in my coat sleeve. The shooting pain came and went, but the itching never stopped. I asked a stranger where I could find the bus station and made my way to the other end of town. I parted with the Glock and spare magazines in case I was searched and bought a Greyhound ticket back to Beaufort. The bus was crowded and moved slowly. The guy next to me smelled like diesel fuel. He listened to loud music on his headphones and wore a zipped-up parka that spilled over into my seat and rubbed against my gunshot wound.

I rested my head against the window and stared at the gray highway. I didn't sleep.

When I got to Beaufort, I found a tourist diner and ordered a cheeseburger and a hot bowl of tomato soup. The waitstaff kept their eyes on me, refilling my ice water and coffee to keep me from dashing. I didn't burden them with my presence any longer than I had to. I walked out to a public park. The Spanish moss shuddered in the wind. I sat beneath an oak tree on a metal park bench that reminded me of Ita and I started to cry. The most beautiful memories I have are still so ugly.

The hot food and coffee gave me some alertness, a little clarity if not strength which kept me from passing out. I sat and did nothing for hours. I watched snowbird couples who hadn't made it to Florida wander along the stone paths, doing their anemic little exercises. I saw a few drug deals go down by the public restroom and, for a moment, got interested but decided to conserve my money. Doing meth would only remind me of Ita even more. There was a No-Smoking sign bolted to the center of the bench. I scooted over to cover it with my back and took out my pack of cigarettes. My lighter was dying. I cupped the flame from the coastal wind. I smoked and wiped my tears. I noticed a white, tourist carriage across the road ahead between stoplights and the general store. There were horse-drawn carriages all over the Southeast from Atlanta to Palm Beach. The horse pulling this temporarily unoccupied carriage was that stocky, thick-footed Belgian breed: the same horse I imagined my possibly fictitious ancestor riding across the scorched flats of the Indian Territory. Is this where I had seen the horse in the first place?

32

got a cheap room off the highway where I holed up for a few days with a bottle of Everclear and a roll of gauze. I didn't know how good the stitch job was. I had nothing to compare it to. I let the grain alcohol wash over my wound straight from the bottle. I didn't know what I was doing. I took vitamins and drank green juice from the health food store as if that would keep me alive longer. I cut the Everclear with Dr. Pepper as I watched the news at night. No mention of the cemetery shooting in Myrtle Beach. Strange how that happens sometimes. The massacre at the Algodon was still top news, probably because a cop was found tied up and shot to death with Kalashnikov rounds. The news anchors said they suspected cartel activity, probably because that's where Ita was found, a dead Latina who didn't have a record of existing anywhere else before. The news didn't mention my fake I.D. as Jeb Ruggins or the forged Loquellos passport, but they had to have found them. It wouldn't take long before they'd link the shooting at the Outer Banks and the sketches in the motel windows with the descriptions of the Indiana Man in Black. Or maybe I was wrong. Ita told me once that I gave the cops too much credit. The news shows played footage of old people in the area saying things like "that just doesn't happen around here." I smoked alone in the TV glow.

I showered up and, in the dead of night, carried my clothes across the street to the 24-hour laundromat where I sat in my white undershirt and an old pair of Ita's gym shorts. There was a neon palm tree next to a Barbadian flag in the window. The air smelled of dryer sheets and Tide. The floor was covered in lint. Half-read newspapers covered the counters and washing machines. I waited to put my stuff in the dryer before having a smoke outside on the curb.

I slept through the next day and woke up fresh and sober at sunset. I put on my clean clothes and walked to the parkway.

I needed a new gun.

I couldn't go back to the gun shops; there was too much heat and it was impossible to get around all the fractured islands without a car.

I bought a hard pack of good cigarettes (American Spirit), something I could offer a street hustler to start a conversation. It was easy to get a piece on the low as long as you had the money. I went through two people before I finally got to a small trailer in the pines where a white guy with an eagle tattooed on his neck sold me a black Sig Sauer. He told me the model's name. It looked like a Glock to me. I asked him if he had a 1911 or a revolver. He shrugged and said he had what he had. He threw in a spare magazine but he never included the bullets for his safety and wrote down the name of the ammunition on a sticky note for me: 9 x 19mm Parabellum.

I bought two boxes of ammunition from a place called Gander Mountain in an upscale strip mall. The parking lot was mostly empty except for a few cars and a flock of seagulls picking at the trash. The palms, planted in the mulched oasis medians, were just saplings held up by wooden stakes and black mesh. The man who sold me the bullets had a purple baseball cap with the bill flipped backward and a denim apron. He called me bossman and asked which range I preferred to shoot at. I told him I shot at a friend's fortified yard up in Salt Creek. He gave an odd look as he put the boxes in my hand. They didn't even read my fake I.D. at the register. I loaded up both magazines for the Sig on the hotel mattress. There was a hurricane coming. The local news kept cutting to the weatherman and footage of people in grocery stores buying up cases of bottled water.

I hit the streets and found the guy who pointed me in the right direction for the gun and scored a bag of classic Mexican benzedrine and some Valium so I could sleep. I spent my last dollars stocking up on food and booze and a few extra days in the motel room. After that, I started casing the old apartment where Ita had once been held.

33

It was all the same. The old crew but different girls. Three guards. Two hefty Eurotrash automat rats from an east-block ghetto to whom Beaufort might seem like an island paradise and an ex-con redneck with swamp cabbage and pine needles in his bloodstream. One man at the door. One on the four-by-four smoking patio less than eight feet off the ground. One inside monitoring (torturing) the girls. Tension must have been high after I shot up the club and got caught in Myrtle Beach. They looked scared and they looked tired and that was good enough for me. Fuck it. If I hung out too long like last time they'd get wise again and I was exhausted too.

Let's put an end to this.

I took my shot as soon as I noticed a pizza man going up the stairs and set out behind him. He wasn't even heading to their apartment. I tapped him on the shoulder with the Sig and told him to do what I said. I had him stand in front of the door and knock. I stood out of sight from the peephole with the gun on him. That narrow, little stream of light in the peephole immediately turned black. The doorman was sizing up the sweating, terrified kid with the Papa John's box. I pressed the barrel of the Sig just underneath the glass lens in the door and pushed the kid out of the way. He dropped the pizza and ran back down the stairs. I pulled the trigger and then shot out the lock. The latch was still connected but I pushed through it and finished off the doorman. Two girls started screaming. I shot the redneck in the face and his blood and skin and skull fragments spread across the living room, spraying the three girls. The patio smoker knew what was up as I kicked the broken door halfway shut behind me. Instead of coming inside with his hands up, he dove over the railing. I told the girls I wasn't going to hurt them as I slid the glass and screen aside to the patio. The guy in the leather jacket landed hard on the grass and moved toward the cypress trees. I shot him in the shoulder and he fell flat on his face.

He fumbled with his shoulder holster for his piece.

I crawled over the patio railing and, with my uninjured arm, let myself hang down as low as possible to shorten the fall. My shins absorbed the drop. I stepped over to the Ukrainian and pushed him face up so he could see me and pulled the silver, ivory-handled pistol from his shoulder holster and jammed it into the back of my pants. He had a karambit on his side as well, one of those Indonesian-made hooked knives with the finger loop you see at gun and knife stores because it's scary to look at, and I ripped it off his belt with the sheath.

"Fuck you, kid whore," he said.

I recognized this guy from the old route. He wasn't Ukrainian, he was from Moldova.

"Adrian?" I said. "I remember you. We used to smoke dope and watch movies. Remember me?"

He nodded.

"Take me to your car."

He spat in my face and I pressed my foot on his bleeding shoulder. He screamed loud enough that the last few birds on the telephone wire took off.

"Come on, take me to your car."

I helped him up and limped into the parking lot. A group of kids watched us. I told them to go inside.

We made it to his black Mercedes SUV. I told him to get into the passenger seat.

"You take it."

"No, you're taking me to him."

"To who?"

"The Russian-American guy. The one who talks to me on the phone."

"Who?"

I bashed in his front teeth with the butt of the Sig and shoved him in the car. There was a roll of paper towels on the floor. I handed it to him and told him to keep pressure on the shoulder wound. I had to keep his free hand occupied and I looked around to see if there was anything I could tie it down with. I was running out of time. I knew I would hear sirens at any moment. I told him to lay his free hand flat on the side console. I took the karambit and sank it through the center of his hand, pinning him to the plastic console.

We hit the highway. He showed me where to go. I told him I would let him live if he didn't fuck with me. No one on the road could see us behind the tinted glass.

The paper roll turned bright red against his shoulder and even more blood gushed from his hand down the sides of the console. I asked him where to go and he mumbled under his breath in his heavy accent and nodded slightly through the agony to point toward the highway exit with the bottom of his chin as his face lost color. He led me past swampland and a few open boar-hunting ranges.

"Where are we going, Adrian?"

"I take you to the boss."

"Yeah, the Russian who took over for Piotyr?"

"I'm not fucking with you. He is out here."

He emptied his bowels. I rolled down the window for the stench. The mists grew into a steady rain and soaked the inside of the door.

"I'm dying," he said.

"The hard part's over, Adrian. Life has been a hard road and you did what you had to do."

He nodded his head almost as if the bouncing suspension were the only thing moving his neck.

"I did," he said, weakly.

"It's not your fault. You had to take what was yours."

I patted him on the thigh so I wouldn't cause him any more pain.

"I followed orders," he said. "I was a soldier."

"When you die, Adrian, you know you're going to heaven, don't you? You know?"

He nodded, delirious.

"But you have to tell me the truth to keep from dying in sin," I said.

"I will not lie. We are brothers," he said. "I forgive you."

"You forgive me? That's good. I forgive you."

The roll of paper towels was just a thin, bloody sponge spilling over his hand.

"Where are we going, Adrian?"

He mumbled something that sounded like "portrayal."

"Where are we going, Adrian?"

"Port Royal," he said.

"Where is that?"

"Northpoint Industrial Campus. Building 112. Port Royal Entertainment, LLC. The door has a code to get in. Turn here."

"What's the code? What's the code to the door, Adrian?"

"Building 112. Northpoint. Port Royal."

"I got that Adrian. Building 112. Port Royal Entertainment. What is the code to the door?"

"Four zero eight five."

"Four seven eight five?"

"Four zero eight five."

"Forty. Eighty-five?"

He nodded and closed his eyes.

"Hey, hey."

I shook him awake.

He blinked a few times and stuck his chin out toward the road.

"It's not far," he said. "No more turns. Port Royal. Four zero eight five."

"Yeah, four zero eight five," I said, trying to ingrain it into my memory.

He closed his eyes again and that was it. It could have been me on that girl's couch. He just bled out.

I drove into the industrial park and read building names and plain-looking company logos. I passed a small, ornate pond covered in lily pads and parked in the lot of building 112.

There was a floating pump among the lily pads anchored to a motor on the bank meant to push up the scummy pond water like a decorative fountain but the flow had slowed to a trickle. The place was a ghost town. I left Adrian's stinking, bloody corpse in the Mercedes and replaced the magazine in the Sig. I checked Adrian's gun, counting the rounds in the mag, sliding one into the chamber. The extra pistol would give me some firepower. I could waste a whole magazine if I had to shoot through a door, or buy myself some distance, before conserving the shots in the Sig Sauer.

I pulled open the glass door beaded with rain and walked into the sterile lobby. There was a small directory by the elevator. I saw it listed plain as day: Port Royal Entertainment, LLC. I took the stairs and entered a small, carpeted hallway. It was quiet except for the humming of the vents. I approached the solid door to the suite and punched the key code. The LED light turned green and I heard the lock release. I walked into another hallway, wider this time. There was even less sound inside. I took the pistol out from underneath my shirt and stepped past a few open office doors. The desks were bare; the rooms were empty. I passed through a dining area with a few microwaves and a fridge. I flicked the lights on and off a few times and looked through the windows at the rainfall. Dust covered the countertops. I pressed up against the wall and tried to slow my heartbeat and at the same time listened for anything in the hall.

I heard nothing.

I moved down the hall to the last trio of glass-enclosed offices. I heard fingers on a keyboard. I went through at least five scenarios in my head.

I could have been alone with some third-party tech guy who didn't even know who he was working for, whose books he was logging.

I paused.

Silence.

I inched toward the corner office.

More typing.

I stood in front of the glass, still hidden by the gray blinds.

"Adrian? Get your fuckin' ass in here."

I knew the voice.

I turned into the open doorway with the gun pointed at his head. He reached into the desk drawer.

It only took one shot to kill him, right through the side of his forehead. He dropped the tiny pistol and fell back in his rolling chair.

It happened so fast.

We exchanged no words, no long stares. In the end, I had my gun ready and his gun was still in the drawer. I saw little to indicate that he was Russian, or half-Russian, except for a small icon on his desk and a knuckle tattoo. He wore jeans and a button-up shirt. His hair was gray. His face was clean-shaven. His pupils were solid. I checked the remaining offices. We were alone. I wiped my prints off Adrian's gun and left it on his desk. I didn't even know his name. It almost didn't matter to me because it wasn't Piotyr.

34

I have one piece of paper left, so I have to make it count. I open up the hollow Bible I spent hours carving out. I can't even fit the Sig inside the crude rectangle. From Genesis to the gospels, its pages litter the floor all spread out like wet newspaper. I've seen aid trucks with the National Guard in the streets as they searched for missing people. The Parris Island boys next door are long gone. I move the desk away from the window. I try to stay hidden in my dark hole.

The sky hasn't opened up. It looks worse like we're heading for a second round, another approaching storm.

I try to keep these pages as orderly as I can. I numbered the corners and stashed them in a hard, postal folder. I guess the idea is to mail it to someone, somewhere, I don't know who. A church? A newspaper journalist? The cops? A company that prints books?

I'm down to my final cigarette. I drop the pencil fragment and walk away from the page to smoke it on the edge of the mattress. I return once it gets close to the filter, ashing on the watery floor.

What else can I tell you?

That day, I drove the Mercedes to the middle of a flood plain close to the marsh. I removed the karambit with the tactical handle and doused everything with bleach I took from a maintenance closet.

After that, I walked back to Beaufort, stopping halfway at a shrimp shack for a meal I paid for with Adrian's money. A girl at the restaurant looked just like Ita. She was waiting outside by the parking lot for a to-go order. She wore a long floral dress and a green raincoat.

I hung out for a couple of days reading a paperback spy novel and watched TV news about the hurricane and stayed drunk until I couldn't live with the guilt any longer and went out one last time and bought a couple of legal pads and an American Heritage dictionary. I'm sitting alone now rounding out this goddamn thing.

The clouds are gathering. The road's covered in debris. Sirens die in the background. I'll wait until midnight to search the evacuated rooms for something to eat, bits of forgotten clothes, drugs, alcohol, electronics... I'll haunt this place like I'm its only ghost.

The End.

AUTHOR BIO

Connor de Bruler was born in Indiana. He lives in South Carolina.

Made in the USA
Middletown, DE
21 October 2022

13260964R00097